ONE MORE
SPRAY OF PERFUME

Phanzi Bradshaw

Milligan Books   **California**

Published and Distributed by:
Milligan Books, Inc

Cover Design
ClearVision Communications /A3Arts.com

Formatting/Layout
Alpha Desktop Publishing

First Printing, November 2003
10 9 8 7 6 5 4 3 2 1
ISBN 0-9742811-9-0

Milligan Books, Inc.
1425 W. Manchester Ave., Suite C
Los Angeles, California 90047
www.milliganbooks.com
(323) 750-3592

Table of Contents

Acknowledgments 4
Foreword.. 6
About The Author.. 7

Part One... 9
Family Fragrances... 9
In School 26

Part Two 40
Poisonous Perfumes... 40
In The Home 40
Meeting My Husband 43
Blues On Christmas 52
My Wedding Day.. 58
Two Weeks After Wedding 63
Queen For The Day.. 67
Fighting For My Life 68
I Cried For Help And No One Helped................................ 70
Til Death Do Us Part, I Think Not..................................... 72
On The Job... 75
Job Suspension With Five Mouths To Feed 86
My Day In Court.. 87
In The Family 91

Part Three.. 120
Scented For Service 120
In The Home 120
In Samaria... 128
In Judea 140
In My Jerusalem... 148

ACKNOWLEDMENTS

To my LORD, my LIFE, and my SAVIOR, JESUS CHRIST who constantly diffused the fragrances of love, reassurance, resources, encouragement, and support from the beginning of writing this book to the end.

To my dear sisters Patricia Washington and Cynthia Joseph and the fun times we shared as you assisted/escorted me down memory lane. For coercing me to, "Go girl!"

To my sons, Robert R. Chaney III and Terrence B. Chaney Sr. who unselfishly accepted the stigma of being reared by an awkward, unknowledgeable, but loving parent.

To my daughters, Lisa S. Washington, Nadine M. Tiku and Deymienne Bradshaw who gave lavishly of themselves, who prayed, encouraged and affirmed me in the writing of this book.

To my grandchildren, that you may be inspired to know that "You can do all things through Jesus Christ ...."

To my dear friends; Rev. Dr. Carolyn L. Johnson, Earnestine Dobson, Parnetha Monroe, Charles & Mae Blake, Darrin & Judith McAllister, Yvonne Gibson-Johnson, Robert & Lois Blakes, Val R. Pearl, Donald T. Paredes, Charles & Jo Ann Quarles, Tonya Lewis, Linda Mitchem, Barbara Smith, The Overcomers Class, Paula J. Litt, George Fields, Linda Castle, Faredeh Samuels, Major DeBerry, James & Mona Thomas, David & Ethel Lewis, Catherine Taylor, Gwendolyn De Long, Lillie Tatum, Kitty M. Wright, Laura Van Pram, Dr. Sylinder Williams, Monique Varnado, Phyllis Smith, Clifford Gasper, Brenda B. James, Bernadine Wright, Vera Williams,

Dorothy J. Taylor, Keith Washington, and Janice Wicker. Thanks for praying for me, believing in me, feeding me, providing shelter for me, giving financial support, allowing me the opportunity to go forth in the ministry, for exhorting me to believe in the God given talents HE has innately placed in me. Thank you for spraying your own unique fragrance of perfume upon my life.

Foreword

"One More Spray Of Perfume," is a story of a young woman's struggle from being a victim of domestic violence, to becoming an advocate against domestic violence.

It is a true story that is reminiscent of Apostle Paul, whose weakness was transformed by Christ to strength. Phanzi describes real life experiences in a way that is both compelling and entertaining. She introduces a Godly approach to dealing with domestic violence that includes redemption, forgiveness, and deliverance for both the survivor and the perpetrator.

James M. Thomas, Pastor
Living Word Community Church
Los Angeles, California

ABOUT THE AUTHOR

Compelled to write her story while battling with a death threatening illness; Phanzi often thought that she would not be here to see the completed work. The mere fact that she is on this side of the living is truly a testament to God's amazing healing, goodness, and mercy.

Phanzi is the mother of five children, and the grand-mother of eleven grandchildren. She has an earned Bachelor and Master's Degree in Theology. For several years, she was employed at one of the largest churches in Los Angeles, California in the capacity of a Christian Counselor, and as Director of Social Services.

Under the leadership of the Holy Spirit, Phanzi has traveled to five of the world's continents spreading the message of God's love and compassion for HIS people. In addition to being a gifted author, Phanzi has the unique talent of exhorting people to their potential in Christ.

PART ONE

FAMILY FRAGRANCES

God sets the solitary in families   Psalms 68:6a NKJV

Being the youngest of three daughters had its advantages. I was catered to and tolerated more than my two sisters. Mae was five years older than me, and Pat and I were exactly thirteen months apart. Mother explained to me that at the age of four months, I began a long battle with asthma—a battle that did not end until I was ten years old. Asthma is a very debilitating sickness. As asthma continued to ravage my body, I weighed only sixty-four pounds from age four to age ten. Mother said I did not get all the discipline that I deserved, because the doctors did not know if the asthma attacks were brought on by emotional stimulation or by an allergic reaction to my environment. Being the youngest, and being chronically ill did have its advantages.

The flip side to this scenario is that anytime anyone got into mischief, I was blamed. As a little girl, it appeared to me that I was always being blamed, corrected, or punished for SOMETHING or just ANYTHING! My sisters would lie on me to keep the heat off of them. Mother believed most of the accusations, because she said I had acquired a nasty little habit of using my illness to my advantage, and manipulating the family on my behalf. To some extent she was right. But I did not do all the things that I was accused of. Marking up the eyes of my Uncle John's US Army picture—guilty. Scrapping food that I did not want to eat behind the refrigerator—guilty. Giving the dog a haircut with scissors, marking the bathroom walls with crayons, pulling an excessive amount of toilet tissue from the roll and streaming it all over the floor, pouring nut brown face powder outside the back door—not guilty.

Occasionally, Mother had meetings with my sisters and me when issues would arise about chores and schooling. I remember one meeting in particular, when Mother tried to discuss the menstrual cycle. In this particular meeting she was hesitant, not as vocal as she normally was. She mumbled and searched for words to use. Later on in life, I realized that her hesitancy stemmed from embarrassment.

Thoughtfully, Mother supplied each of us with a paperback booklet that explained the twenty-eight day cycle of an unfertilized egg in a female's body. When everyone was finished reading their pamphlet, the meeting reconvened, and the discussion began. Mother asked each of us to repeat back what we had read in our own words. Mae and Pat did the same amount of incoherent mumbling. Mother became indignant, and told my sisters that she did not know why they were going to school if they could not explain what they had read. She then decided to compare my ability to comprehend what I had read with my sisters' awkwardness. Mother always said, "I was her precocious child." Even at seven years of age I was able to explain what I read in the book, and basically got my Mother off the hook, because she was too ashamed to talk about a woman's body and sexual issues with us.

My diet left a lot to be desired. I absolutely detested vegetables, green or yellow. Mother cooked a lot of vegetables, and would insist that I eat all of them because "Carrots will make you have pretty eyes, and the green vegetables are just good for you." Did I buy her reasoning? I think not. My bouts with asthma decreased my appetite. In order to see that I ate a sufficient amount of vegetables, Mother made every effort to

10

cook balanced meals. She would sit with me long after meals were over, attempting to encourage me to eat all of the vegetables, meat, salad or whatever was served.

There were foods that I definitely preferred. My favorite foods were milk, pork chops, hot chocolate, and a half slice of bread. I remember this one occasion that Mother cooked okra. I was so repulsed by okra, that the mere smell of it cooking upset my stomach. It was slimy, and while it was cooking it looked "yucky." To my eyes okra had to be one of the most gross undesirable, unappealing vegetables that God ever made. Amazingly, in later years, I developed a love for okra, cooked in any method—fried, mixed in a succotash with butter beans, tomatoes and corn, sprinkled on top with crowder peas, or just steamed. Now, okra is an all right food with me.

I recall this one occasion that we were scheduled to have a special outing at the Palace Theater to see a colored boy named Sugar Child Robinson. Sugar Child was, billed at the Palace Theater as a "genius." Genius, because he was a colored child that had the unique gift of playing the piano without any formal music lessons. He was a mystery to both white and colored folks.

It was commonly reported and publicized that he could neither read music, nor words. As I sat at the kitchen table Mae and Pat urged me to eat the okra, that it really wasn't that bad. They coached me to hold my breath, take a huge mouthful, and swallow. I followed their instructions, but their plan didn't work for me, my stomach would not cooperate. I became nauseous and I spat the okra out. This went on for about an hour, and it was too late for us to catch the bus downtown.

As I realized how disappointed my sisters were that we did not get the opportunity to see "Sugar Child," I felt rather bad that I could not keep the okra down. When I questioned them they said they were discontented that our trip was canceled, but they were upset with Mother. Their feeling toward me were indulgent and understanding.

There was also the incident of carrying the lunch bag to school. My siblings had books to carry each day. I had no books issued in both the first and second grades. Mother's natural decision was that I'd carry the lunch for all of us. I didn't want to carry the lunch because it was normally packed in a huge brown paper bag, twisted at the top, I suppose to assist me in carrying it, and further secured with a huge long piece of cord string. Each morning, I would complain to my Mother that my sisters never had to carry the unattractive bag. Most of the other students carried their lunches in a neat little lunch box, but I had to carry an old twisted-top brown paper bag with either a string or a piece of rag securing it to further embarrass me.

Each morning as we approached Hickory Street, I would announce to my sisters that I was no longer going to carry the bag, and unceremoniously drop the bag of sandwiches in the middle of the sidewalk and walk away. Mae and Pat would become very upset with me and plead with me to pick up the bag. This request fell on deaf ears, and I would continue down Hickory Street to school. In utter desperation, Mae and Pat would knock on the door of one of our relatives, Cousin Louise, who lived on Hickory Street and tell her what I had done. Cousin Louise was a real jovial woman, who had an excellent sense of humor. In my child's mind, she was always wearing an apron over her dresses, or a white uniform as she was on the Usher Board at church. After their desperate explanation of what had transpired, she would laugh out real loud, and call me to her. She would say, "Little cousin your sisters and your Mom are depending on you to carry every-one's lunch to school." She continued, "All of you will be hungry at lunch time, if you don't pick that bag up out of the street, and be the lunch carrier for the day." Somehow, in her soft, jovial manner, she'd encourage me to pick up the lunch bag and carry the lunch to school. Whenever Cousin Louise would enter in to resolve my siblings' problems, I'd consent to carry the lunch bag the rest of the way to school.

Mae and Pat would really become angry with me, when they would find me at school to retrieve their sandwiches and fruit. I would have torn open a hole in the side of the brown paper bag, retrieved and eaten all of the meat in the sandwiches, leaving them with fruit, bread and mayonnaise for lunch. Upset with me? Yes they were, as a matter of fact, my sisters were angry, disgusted, and hungry, because of my actions. Finally they reported this behavior to my Mother who immediately placed the rod of correction on my behind, ridding me of this mistake for the rest of our time at school. The next year I received my own set of books to carry, thereby making it each individual's responsibility to carry their own lunch.

My paternal grandmother lived with us in uptown New Orleans. Nanny's real name was Nancy Bradshaw. Often in the mornings, before we girls were awake, she'd prepare a breakfast of thin cut pork chops, grits, scrambled eggs, homemade biscuits, and a tomato gravy. Mae, Pat, and I were awakened by the smell of freshly baked biscuits, the aroma filling the house. Even my poor eating habits were stimulated at the smell of Nanny's cooking. We would scramble to the kitchen table, and sit down waiting to eat the delicious breakfast she had prepared. Nanny had long slender fingers, and she would point that index finger at us saying, "No, no, my three beautiful black queens, you have not washed your face, nor brushed your teeth. Queens just do not behave themselves in this manner."

Occasionally, Nanny would sit in her rocking chair in her room, smoking her pipe filled with Prince Albert tobacco. There she would impart to us knowledge of our ancestry. She did not have any recollection of her grandmother or grandfather. Strangely enough, she had imperfect memory of her Mother; however she did remember her Daddy, Papa Joe. That was my great-grandfather Joe, who she said was a blacksmith. But Uncle Cornelius, daddy's brother, Nanny called "a shame and disgrace to all his people." Later on I realized that Nanny had this terrible opinion of Uncle Cornelius because he was always drinking alcohol. She said, "my son is a fool and a shame to me!" The reason Nanny had this opinion of Uncle Cornelius was that when he drank and became drunk he would go in the shed located at the rear of our house and yell out crying that no one loved him. Uncle Cornelius would go into the shed, and no one knew he was there until he began to yell out, "Help, Help me somebody, no one loves me." Once when Uncle Cornelius was in the back shed drunk, he urinated on Mother's winter clothings she had stored there during the summer. Nanny was ashamed, while Mother was repulsed and disgusted.

The nickname Nanny gave us all was "Black Queens." She said that we were treated and raised like the little white children that she baby-sat for, when she cleaned their parents' homes, she said the only difference is that we had the misfortune of being born Black.

We lived in the uptown section of New Orleans, called pension town because most of the residents were retired and receiving their pensions from the Southern Pacific Railroad. The house we lived in consisted of a living room, two bedrooms, kitchen, bathroom, and a screened porch that served as a third bedroom for the three girls. The front of the house had a porch that extended across its width, and a wonderful front porch swing.

My sisters and I spent many hours enjoying that swing. I especially enjoyed swinging in the front porch swing at dusk dark. As the evening sun would begin to set and darkness appeared, the "lightning bugs" would appear out of nowhere. I would enter into an imaginary state of mind as the smell of night jasmines filled the thick humid air. I would swing and think of other places in this world, that I would like to visit, or places like where Heidi and her Elm-Uncle lived in the mountains, or places I'd hear described on the radio as we listened to the news.

The house we all lived in was a "shotgun" house—one room built straight on the end of another room. None of the rooms were independent. Standing at the front door of a "shotgun" house, you could look straight through to the back door. Whenever visitors, came to the front door, they would have to walk through Mother and Daddy's room to use the restroom. When people knew that Daddy was working at night, it was commonplace to enter the house using the side alley. It is an acceptable practice in New Orleans to entertain one's guests in the kitchen. Mother and Daddy slept in the front bedroom, which was directly behind the living room. Then there was a huge hallway closet on one side of the hall, and the bathroom on the other side of the hall. Next to the hallway was Nanny's room, followed by the kitchen, and the half-screen, half-wood back porch, where my sisters and I slept.

During the mid forties it was safe to sleep on such a back porch without fear of break-ins. There were times when the weather was extremely hot and humid, and we slept with the front door ajar. The only security was a small latch that secured the screen door. Unfortunately, now we have to resort to security systems, motion detectors, security bars, deadbolts and iron fences. And with all this high-tech security, we are still very vulnerable and insecure.

Living in the 21st century is cause for children to be afraid. The scariest time I can remember as a child in New Orleans, was the night my Mother took us to see "Dr. Frankenstein" at the Roxy Theater. The movie was very scary, and as we were putting our gowns on for the night, Mother having gone over The Lord's Prayer with us, we were kissed, the lights turned off, and put to bed. I expressed my fears to my Mother. I told her that the movie had frightened me, and I was fearful of sleeping on the back porch. She responded, "That was a movie, and nothing is going to harm you. Your sisters are here with you, Nanny is one room away, and Daddy and I are in our bedroom." I got one more reassuring kiss, and the lights were turned out. Hurriedly, I covered my head with the sheets.

My imagination was working overtime that night. I could hear footsteps in the alleyway, and as I peered from beneath the covers and looked outside the window, the wind rattled the leaves of the plum tree in the backyard. Hearing the leaves brush against each other further increased my aggravation and fear. The leaves cast shadows on the walls and they looked like Dr. Frankenstein, ghosts and goblins from the graveyard, just like a scene in the movie. This time these invaders were in my bedroom to take me away!

Reluctantly, shivering under the covers, I cried out to my sisters. My voice was just above a whisper, but they both were sound asleep. I kept calling, "Mae, Pat, will somebody help me? I am afraid the monsters will eat me up." In sheer desperation, I screamed at the top of my voice, HELP, HELP, the monsters are coming in the window!!!" Immediately both my sisters hopped out of their bed, and called out, "Baby, what is the matter?" I was crying uncontrollably by then. Mother, Daddy, and Nanny soon bolted in our room. With uncontrollable sobs, I managed to tell my parents someone was in the alley. Daddy quickly went to the kitchen and retrieved his flashlight. He appeared back in our room, and his hand was in his robe pocket. In later years, I came to realize that he had a gun in his robe pocket. He left out the back door and investingated the alley.

Upon his return, he reported that no one was in the alley. Then, Daddy picked me up in his arms and, through sobs, I told them about the ghosts, goblins, Dr. Frankenstein, they were hovering right outside. They were trying to get me! As I was being held in Daddy's arms, Mother began to stroke my back and neck and talk to me and explain that what I saw was a reflection that had been caused by the moon shining on the trees, casting shadows on the walls of our room. She demonstrated what she meant by turning off the lights, then turning them on again, thus proving that no ghosts or goblins were present.

Nanny began to scold Mother for taking us to a scary movie, because I was only five years old and could not understand the difference between real and imaginary. Mother became indignant and defensive and told Nanny, "When did you become an expert on child rearing? You left your only two sons for someone else to bring up!" Nanny's expression changed as she dropped her head. Daddy intervened by telling Mother and Nanny, "Let's put Baby in the bed with us, and table this discussion." That night, feeling secure between Mother and Daddy, I slept the entire night through without incident.

Mother often told us if it was in her power, but she would build us our own little world, supply it with our every heart's desire, and fence the little world in so that we would be sheltered from the cruel world. She was not financially sound enough to do that, but she did manage to shelter us from the devastation of segregation. When Mother would take us to hospitals, visiting her friends, or to church, and it was necessary to ride the New Orleans Public busses and streetcars (trolley). I remember questioning my parents as to, why there was a screen, and why we could we only sit behind the screen? She would, very quickly and softly, tell us, "Those seats are for white folks only." I never questioned my Mother's response. Somehow her fear was transmitted to us, and we accepted her answer. Those seats are for "white folks only."

It was not that I lacked intellect. I saw the water fountains that were marked "for colored only," and the large water cooler fountains marked, "for whites only." Elaborate numerous seating was provided at the lunch counters "for whites only," while small limited seating in the rear of the store was marked "for colored only". I saw large beautiful restaurants where the

Greyhound busses stopped, that were marked "for whites only." I had to go to the rear of the restaurant, marked "for colored only", and be served food that was wrapped in newspaper. The restrooms that were very white and sanitary looking were marked "for whites only," and the outside toilets, that you could smell long before you arrived were marked "for colored only".

Considering what I know now, and what I've come to realize about the whole horrid segregation experience, I fully comprehend Mother's position. She tried to protect us from hurt, harm, and danger under a cruel inequitable system that was based upon the color of one's skin. When Mother said that these privileges or services were "for white folks", in my childlike innocence, I trusted my parents' explanation.

Hatred, bigotry, separatism were not taught in our home. Consequently, my sisters and I were protected from a lot of discriminatory practices.

There were times that Mother worked to help our family's financial position, and to buy her three girls beautiful clothing, toys, and shoes. I recall when she worked for an affluent white family in New Orleans. Her job description, from 8:00AM until 4:00PM, was to clean the house, mop and wax the floors, vacuum the carpets, wash, starch, hang up and take in the clothing from off the line in the backyard, iron all of the family's clothing, baby-sit the children, answer the door and telephone, take messages and cook a full-course meal. For all of this strenuous work, she was paid three dollars per day, or fifteen dollars per week. These wages were considered to be top wages in the early fifties and late forties.

Mother came home from work one evening enraged. She complained that she had been ironing clothing in the basement. When lunchtime approached, Mrs. Muntz, her "boss lady," summoned her for lunch. Mother had sprinkled two more starched white business shirts and put them in the refrigerator, and wanted to finish the hard ironing before she ate lunch.

After washing shirts, the procedure in those days was to prepare the cooked starch, and immerse the shirts in the starch, then hang them out to dry. Prior to ironing, they would be sprinkled with water, rolled up to keep them damp, and set in the refrigerator so that the hot humid New Orleans weather would not dry them out again. Now we have instant spray starch.

Mother said, she approached the basement stairs leading to the Muntz's kitchen and there she saw a sandwich that she assumed had been prepared for her. It had been left on the stairs. The sandwich was surrounded by flies and roaches. Mother said even though she was hungry, she did not eat the food. She said, "I can deal with the disproportion of work versus pay, but I will not have you treating me worse than you do your family dog!"

When Mother's week was over at the Muntzs, she did not return to their job, nor did she return their telephone calls. I felt real good about her making a decision and taking a stand against inhumane treatment. Besides that I really enjoyed Mother being home when I got off the school bus. Nanny was fine to receive me from school, but I missed Mother's warm hugs and kisses, asking me what I learned today.

Mondays were special days for the "three black queens," Mae, Pat, and Pansy. From June until September, there was no school it was summer vacation. Monday was Daddy's day off from work. Bimonthly, on the first and the fifteenth of the month were his paydays and on the Mondays following his pay period, he would travel to downtown New Orleans to pay his bills. These occasions were special to us in that we got to travel with Daddy.

Mother would dress us in pretty pastel colored dresses with perfectly starched and ironed white pinafores over the dresses. Mae's dress was pastel yellow, Pat's pastel blue, and mine a pastel pink. These were dresses Mother purchased from Mark Isaacs, one of the few department stores that allowed

19

"coloreds" to open a charge account. Mae's dress was different from Pat's and mine. Her dress had rows of ruffles in the back. When she donned the starched and ironed pinafore over the dress, the rows of ruffles appeared in the back of the dress under the buttons that closed it. Pat and I, because of our close proximity in age, and because it was stylish at that time, were dressed in the same design of dress, but different colors.

Our outings included, thespian performances, the Delgado Museum, the Audubon Park Zoo, and the New Orleans Philharmonic Symphony. Whoever was appearing at the Municipal Auditorium on Daddy's day off, there we would be.

Daddy probably had no idea what he was imparting in our lives. Years ago when he was a much younger man, he sustained an injury when a train rolled over his right leg; he still walked with a limp due to improper and inadequate medical care. He was removed from his family due to the inequity and depravity bred by slavery and segregation. He was born three generations after the Emancipation Proclamation was signed, which allegedly freed the slaves from their bondage, but it gave no provision or allowance for the inbred dependence blacks still had on whites for their livelihood.

Impoverished because he had no education, nor opportunity to work for his living. Hardships, because due to the total devastation of slavery and segregation his Mother, Nanny, did not raise him. She left Alexandria, Louisiana for New Orleans in search of employment so that she could take care of her family, leaving Daddy and Uncle Cornelius with her half sisters, and other distant relatives.

Unfortunately the money that Nanny sent for Daddy's clothing, food, and other expenses never directly benefited him. Daddy recalled to us that he was treated as a slave in his Aunt's home. He was required to go in the snow and gather the cows, when he had no shoes to wear. Clean up after all his aunt's daughters, pick cotton, plant and maintain the garden, and not given adequate food to satisfy his hunger were just a few injustices he was subjected to. Daddy recalled his feet being so cold that he lost the feeling in them, and sometimes when his chores led him outside in the bitter, cold, weather, he would drive the cows out of their warm sitting places to warm his bare feet.

When he exposed us to the cultural, theatrical, and musical world, it was his way of affording us the privileges that as a child he never was afforded. Daddy loved music. On special holidays like Thanksgiving and Christmas, he would sit at the piano, and pick out the melodies of Christmas carols and gospel songs. Songs like "Nearer my God to Thee," "Just a closer walk with Thee," "Amazing Grace," "Silent Night," "Hark the Herald angels sing," without ever having had one music lesson. He was gifted from God to listen to music and play the melody on the piano. Thus, his God given talent, and his love for music gave his "three black queens" the love of music.

Daddy was of medium height, mild mannered and soft spoken. Because of the effects that slavery and segregation had on the African American community, and on the family structure, the only schooling Daddy had was to the second grade. Daddy was reared in several towns in Alexandria, Louisiana and a little town called Colfax, Louisiana.

He loved to laugh and have fun with his daughters, tickling us, swinging us around and around so that when we were turned loose, we were very disoriented and dizzy.

Daddy very rarely had the privilege of attending church with his family. His vigorous six days a week, twelve hours a day work schedule only permitted him one day off, Mondays. I do remember one Sunday afternoon, we all dressed and went to an afternoon service at our church, New Salem Missionary Baptist Church. Rev. Wilson, our pastor, preached and was extending the invitation for the congregation to join the church or become Christians.

Surprisingly Daddy began to sing his favorite song, "Shine On Me," and rose from his seat to accept the minister's challenge to become a Christian and become a member of the church. Tears poured down his dimpled, ebony face. I was so proud of my Daddy. Caught up in the excitement and wanting to share this moment with him, I sprang from my seat, ran up and grabbed Daddy by his pant leg, holding real tight and hugging his leg. The entire church was overjoyed, as Daddy sang every verse over and over again. Mother, Mae, and Pat were all touched by this experience and in a show of love, admiration, respect, and support the entire family joined Daddy at the altar.

Rev. Wilson, completely confused, had to decide why the entire family was responding to the call to become a Christian. Mother he knew was already converted. Mae and Pat had confessed their faith in Jesus Christ and were baptized. He looked at us strangely. I suppose in his mind he said what in the world is happening here? Daddy completed his song. Without explanation, Mother, Mae and Pat returned to their seats. A sigh of relief came from Rev. Wilson as he extended a handshake to my Dad and me.

Now I had no idea that my getting up to stand with Daddy would be interpreted as I wanted to accept Jesus Christ, and be baptized, but it did, and therefore Daddy and I were baptized, and became members of New Salem Missionary Baptist Church. Did I fully understand what I had done? Yes, I knew that I believed in the Lord Jesus Christ to save my soul from an eternal burning hell. All of the other beliefs, standards of conduct, and teachings, were taught later on in life. Well, when church was over Daddy and I received congratulatory hugs, kisses and handshakes from the members of the congregation.

As we walked home from church, Mae, Pat, and I talked unceasingly about the actual baptism. My sisters were schooling me on what to expect. They shared that first, I would have to pray and ask the Lord if He had really saved my soul, and to ask Him for a confirmation in a dream. Then I'd have to share the dream or vision with the entire congregation. This was somewhat scary to me, so I asked my sisters, what if he didn't give me anything to say? Both of them assured me that during this period of prayer I would be given something to share with the congregation.

They chattered on about me having to wear a white long dress, have my head tied up with a white scarf, and right before I was to be lifted in the pool, the deaconess would tie my dress down at my feet to prevent the water from getting under my dress and lifting it in the pool. Pat began to mimic the preacher and said, "I have here this little sister Pansy, and upon the profession of her faith in the Lord Jesus Christ, I baptize you in the name of the Father, Son, and nanny goat!" Mae, Pat, and Daddy roared with laughter, as Pat imitated the preacher.

Strangely, Mother was unusually quiet during the walk to our home. When we arrived, Mother asked Daddy, "Why is it that the few occasions that we are afforded to attend church together as a family, every time the preacher extends an invitation to join church you go to the altar? And did you have to sing every verse over and over again?" She was upset, because Daddy's actions were embarrassing to her. Daddy countered, "O honey, I just felt the Lord moving in my heart!" Mother wanting to have the last word said," But do you have to sing the same old tired song, sing every verse, then sing it repeatedly?" This exchange of words was one of the few times I ever heard Mother and Daddy argue, or disagree. I figured maybe there was some pretense of virtue on both parents' part, or maybe there were things discussed that I didn't know. Mother certainly did not know how the Lord was motivating Daddy, and Daddy perhaps needed to control his emotions. As I reflected on the incident, taking into account that Daddy had done the same thing a couple of times in the past, it was both amusing and distressing.

Mother was from a small town in Louisiana, just outside of Donaldsonville, called Abend—Louisiana. Named because the entire town is located in extreme curves on the River Road. The Greyhound bus ride to visit my maternal grandparents was always special. Mother would pack our clothing, fry several chickens, make sandwiches of ham and cheese. Bring homogenized milk for us to drink and bake cakes to take for us to eat while we rode the bus to visit Poppa, and Mama Baba. This again was Mother's technique to shelter my sisters and me from a racist segregated society. She cooked the food for us to carry with us so we wouldn't have to be subjected to prejudiced restaurants serving inferior foods.

York and Victoria Langs Jenkins lived in Abend. Poppa raised chickens, cows, pigs and horses. During our rides to Abend, we would see many cows and horses, and in our childish minds we attributed ownership of all the animals to Poppa.

Poppa was a small built man with white hair. He was a preacher. God had uniquely gifted him with total recall of the word of God, even though he was unable to naturally read or write his own name. Mama Baba was short and stout. She always wore an apron, because she was always cooking something good to eat. On one of our visits, she had cooked some type of meats, and smothered it in a red gravy. Without tasting as much as a teaspoon, I asked, "What in the world is that mess Mama Baba is cooking?" Certainly she didn't expect me to eat it! When the mess was completely cooked, Mother insisted I taste a very small amount. The mess was delicious, and I ate two bowls! Mama Baba would often remind me that she would be cooking another one of her messy dishes.

There were times when we would spend the last two weeks prior to school opening at my grandparents' home. To give Mother a break, Mama Baba would suggest that Mother go home to see about Daddy. However, because of persistent bouts with asthma, and inadequate medical facilities, in that part of Louisiana she would not leave me.

During our visits, we would sometimes see Poppa milk and run the cows. Poppa had a name for every one of his chickens, cows, and horses, and communicated with them as if they could comprehend what he was demanding of them. Inevitably, it was time to return to New Orleans and re-enroll in school.

Fortunately school was always a pleasurable experience for me. There were times that I was unable to attend due to illness, but ordinarily I enjoyed attending.

In School

As we were slowly eating and savoring a bag lunch which consisted of a peanut butter and jelly sandwich with milk, Mr. Dorest, our sixth grade teacher, called me and several other students and requested us to stay after school for a few minutes. He suggested that we could take the last school bus home. Anxiously, I awaited the 3:00 P.M. closing bell to alert us that the school day had come to an end. Mr. Dorest was also McDonogh #32 School's music director. As he gathered us together, he brought out a script and sheet music to some song. He had each of us read the script, and then with meticulous patience he taught each of us the song, "Tis the Voice of the Lobster." Later, we were to discover that Mr. Dorest had been requested by the Principal of the main campus of McDonogh #32 School to include some of the children at our annex location in auditioning for parts in a school play that the school was presenting in the summer of 1954.

All of the finalists from our annex school (converted naval barracks) would be brought to the main campus where judges would critique our performance. A final decision would be made by these judges as to who would be cast in a play called, "Alice's Adventures in Wonderland" by Lewis Carroll.

The annex of the McDonogh # 32 was a part of the Algiers Naval Station. These barracks and offices were converted to accommodate grades K-6, due to increased amounts of colored families to the area, and to perpetuate segregation. Most of the children in our section of New Orleans were bused past two all white schools in order to pacify the segregation laws.

Mr. Dorest was very diligent in seeing to it that we were adequately prepared, we not only rehearsed the lines for the characters we were selected to audition for we also knew the other characters lines so that we knew when we were cued to speak for our role.

After lunch each day, all the children who were participating in the auditions, were summoned to a classroom which housed an old brown upright Baldwin piano, that had some keys missing and the ivory worn off others. Mr. Dorest often commented on how the piano was in need of a good tuning. He was a jovial fat man who had the touch of an accomplished artist on the keyboard. Even though some of the notes struck sounded off-key, somehow the continuity, timing, and melody, mixed with his musical expertise, created sounds that were beautiful, even from an antiquated, beat up, out-of-tune piano.

Miss Jones, the ranking teacher at the annex was a plain-looking, skinny, pale complexioned woman. Whenever she spoke she always enunciated pronouncing words with great care and diction. Miss Jones was always immaculately dressed, either in a suit with a choker-collared blouse, or dresses that dragged the floor when she walked. Miss Jones wore her hair neatly combed to the back with a tightly twisted bun.

Mr. Dorest seemed to put more emphasis on my singing role than he did with any of the other children. Sing, sing, sing, was all I was requested to do! He did not focus on my speaking parts for my character, Alice. There were even times when the other children who were auditioning were allowed to play for recess, but I was to sing, sing, sing! Sometimes I'd miss a note, as I was distracted staring out the window, as the children played. Enviously, I watched as the children played games of jump rope, hopscotch, red light, and jacks. By the time I was eight years old, I could beat all my friends; Carol, Jennifer, Clifford, Veronica, Judy, none of them was a match for me. Now that I had made my ninth birthday, I was the undisputed champion player of jacks, and I could not go to play to defend my championship.

Charles, Junior, Bernadette, Geraldine, and I were not required to do the normal class work assigned to the other children who were not auditioning. All that was necessary for us was to show up at school, and from the opening bell until lunchtime, we practiced, occasionally taking ten minutes breaks and stopping for lunch. Lunch was normally one hour. The auditioning group lunch was abbreviated to twenty minutes to consume the normal peanut butter and jelly sandwich, and milk. Then we were to report back to the room where we practiced.

Finally, the day arrived that the audition was to take place on the main campus. My entire body was an emotional mine-field. I was so excited, relieved, and anxious. Excited, that I could finally go outside and play with all the rest of my school-mates, after being confined in rehearsals for more than three months, five days a week, rehearsing song after song. Relieved, that the day had finally arrived that a decision would be made as to who would be selected to play the lead role of Alice.

When we arrived at the other colored campus it was lunchtime, and the children were playing in the yard. How very different their facility was from ours! They had swings, monkey bars, and a wonderful merry go round. At our campus, there were no monkey bars, merry go rounds, or swings. We had to become creative in our recess, and play time, and deal with games that were imaginative, such as Simon Says, Redlight, Jacks.

Their campus was a huge complex consisting of three buildings built in a U-shape. Inside the U was the playground, almost completely surrounded by the three dark brown buildings trimmed in a bright yellow, and large exit/entrance doors painted with bright red paint. Our campus was archaic in comparison. Our buildings were naval barracks converted into classrooms, painted a sickly and dreary gray. Their campus had a cafeteria, which served hot meals. Our daily lunches consisted of a cold peanut butter and jelly sandwich and cold milk. They sat at long tables and benches with each table decorated with a small vase of flowers made from various colors of crepe paper. We sat at tables and benches painted the same ghastly gray with no pretty vases of flowers.

When it became necessary for our teacher to address the entire student body, we stood in line in the hot sun, while the ranking teacher addressed us with a bullhorn to amplify the sound. Their campus had a public address system, so the Principal, could inform the student body of changes from the comfort of his office, while the students were seated in the classroom at their desks.

The grounds on the front of the main campus were meticulously landscaped, with rows of gladiolas, sweet peas, and bird of paradise flowers surrounding the green shrubbery. Their front lawn was covered with lush green St. Augustine grass, the concrete walkway lined with green hedges that led to the big red double entry doors. At our naval barracks we had asphalt and concrete with no flower, nor shrubbery. Occasionally we were treated to games of softball, whenever someone would become inventive and make a bat out of a branch from a tree and a ball out of pieces of yarn and rags tied tightly together.

Much to my surprise, we were not greeted with open arms and cheers of welcome from the main campus students. We were teased, insulted, and mocked, generally the types of greetings that one comes to expect from children who have not been taught to respect and value others, despite their differences. "Look at the ugly kids from the annex!" "These people look like monkeys from the country," "they sure are ugly, I have not seen one pretty one yet," they cried out adding to our anxiety.

As the rest of the audition hopefuls and I got on the main campus, we were hustled away to a vacant classroom. The classroom was furnished with approximately fifty desks and chairs, a piano, lots of visual aids, the alphabets written in cursive, a bulletin board beautifully decorated with animals and fruits for the border, and displays of student works. Large pots of green plants were on display near the big open

29

windows, along with small paper cups that had small plants growing inside. The plants were lovely and lush and were being nurtured by the sun that streamed in through the windows. In the rear of the classroom, I noticed a brown and white portable record player, beside three stacks of 78s, 45s, and 33 1/3 phonograph records.

We sat down in the desk and chair sets, and waited to be instructed by our teachers as to what to do. While we waited, I talked with Geraldine. Geraldine was auditioning for the role of the Mad Hatter. I confessed to her my fears that perhaps I would not be chosen, and the fear of being rejected and disappointed. Gerry gave me a reassuring hug and said, "You will do just fine, you certainly will be selected as Alice. You have practiced enough, and have perfected every song." I hugged her and told her thanks for the vote of confidence.

A hush fell over the room as Miss Jones, the ranking teacher at the annex, and Mr. Simon, the Principal of McDonogh #32 Elementary School, entered the room. Mr. Simon was a heavy-set man, and appeared to be about five feet wide and five feet high. He wore horn-rimmed eyeglasses that sat on the bridge of his nose. Every time I saw Mr. Simon, he carried a long, round, wooden pointer. Most of the students respected Mr. Simon. He did not carry that pointer only to drive an academic point home on the chalkboard; it was rumored among the students that he would hit your hands for misbehavior.

During my school days corporal punishment was accepted by the educational system, and endorsed by most parents. So wherever Mr. Simon went throughout the main campus or the annex, he received much respect, because his reputation preceded him. Mr. Simon clapped his hands, and that was his signal for the students standing in line outside of the class to form a single line, and join the students already in the class. Twenty or more boys and girls filed into the class.

Approximately twenty to thirty five students were present for the audition, and only ten students would be successful in obtaining main character roles in our production of "Alice's Adventures in Wonderland."

Miss Jones began to welcome us to the main campus, and to tell us the reasons that we were summoned, as if we didn't already know. She bowed her head and prayed, asking the Lord for HIS directions, HIS wisdom, and HIS choice for the characters to be portrayed, Amen.

Mr. Simon came up afterwards and gave a long monotone speech about correct deportment, correct English, and representing our school properly because present at the production would be some white Orleans Parish Board members. After about fifteen minutes of rambling rhetoric, Mr. Simon concluded his speech, and the class broke into thunderous applause. It was not that his speech was so wonderful or encouraging, we were just glad for him to sit down and shut up!

Finally, as we sat eagerly waiting, the judges began to call the name of the character, and then the students' names that were to try out for the character. The first character was the Queen of Hearts; the students auditioning were Barbara, Mary, Helen, Stephanie, and Carol from the #32 annex. The panel of judges consisted of three women teachers and three men teachers: Mr. Johnson, Mr. Webb, Mr. Dorest, Mrs. Christopher, Mrs. Hawkins, and Miss Williams.

When the students' name were called, they stood facing the rest of the tryouts and the judges. One of the judges began to read several lines prior to the characters; it was the tryouts' responsibility to respond to the cue without any prompting from their peers or teachers.

Horrified, I listened as the judges explained to each participant that they would be judged according to their clarity of speech, and retention of their lines. There were very few lines in the script that I had been rehearsed on; all I rehearsed was all of the lyrics and melodies to the songs that I was taught. Sweat poured from my brow, my hands became cold and clammy, my breathing irregular. I didn't exactly lose consciousness, but I came very close.

As my breathing became more labored, my stomach progressed from queasiness into extreme nausea. I excused myself to the ladies' room and there my stomach was relieved. Washing my face with cold water, I peered into the mirror. The reflection that looked back was not the one that I had grown to know over the past nine years. The eyes that I saw were widened, nostrils were flared from excessive breathing, perspiration was still pouring from my brow. Thoughts kept playing in my mind, you are going to be the laughingstock of the school, you only know about ten lines, and these judges are auditioning according to script retention!

Nervously, I attempted to calm myself, and return to the auditioning process. Suddenly, Geraldine burst into the ladies' room calling out to me, "the judges are now ready to do auditions for Alice, they want you now. All of the other tryouts have read, and it appears that the judges favor Barbara."

Barbara was a very pretty girl, with long curly braids down her back, who attended school at the main campus. I was a doubled-dipped chocolate brown complexion with medium length hair, combed into five braids, who attended school at the annex.

Gerry told me that Barbara's retention and diction had been perfect, she didn't miss a cue. I was not already intimidated, this tidbit of information did nothing for my confidence. As we hurried hurried back to the room, Gerry asked," are you all right?" Incoherently, I mumbled something that sounded like, I needed to use the restroom. In the hallway we heard the sounds of music, laughter, and talking, emanating from the classroom. The second we came into view, sounds ceased and it appeared that all eyes were riveted on me.

Miss Williams, the first grade teacher, said, " My God, child, where have you been? We were all waiting for you!" Nervously, I stood before the students and the judges, attempting to regain my composure, for what appeared to be a short time, but obviously to Mr. Dorest it was too long. I heard him clear his throat, and I looked at him and nodded for him to start the piano introduction to "Tis the Voice of the Lobster." The song was sung and completed miraculously, flawlessly.

The classmates and the judges responded by giving me a standing ovation. Mr. Dorest was so pleased with the outcome of my audition, that he stood and announced to the judges that there was one more song that he would like them to hear before their decision was made. Abruptly, Miss Williams, the skinny, lanky, giraffe-looking first grade teacher, interrupted him by informing him that too much time had been spent on this particular finalist, and she desired to hear no more singing, but wanted to cue me by beginning to read the script, to evaluate my grammar, and retention of my lines.

At this point Mr. Dorest requested the rest of the panel of judges to meet him down the hall in the principal's office. Immediately after the teachers left the room, and the noise of a closing door was heard, the other finalists began to speculate as to who would receive the role of "Alice." All of my classmates felt that, even though I had a fine singing voice, Barbara was the winner.

Stella, a girl who attended school at the main campus, stood up and decreed to the entire room, "Barbara is the winner of the Alice role, because Pansy is too black!" The whole class broke out in laughter. I was very hurt and ashamed. Her humiliating remarks continued, "Pansy's hair is nappy and short!" She said Barbara could pass the brown paper bag test. The brown paper bag test was initiated by whites to perpetuate disunity among the Negro race. The basic criteria is that if you were lighter complexioned than a brown paper bag, you were acceptable. If your complexion was darker than the brown paper bag, you were rejected. The essence of this was "If you're white or light, you are all right, if you are brown, stick around, but if you are black, step to the back!" Feeling inferior and hurt I smiled, but inside those words were painful.

In a racist and segregated society, African Americans were constantly bombarded with a sense of being second class citizens. Since the dominant society was white, people of color mistakenly felt that the more white they looked, the more accepted they would be to others. This is a fallacy that has been passed on for generations. Not only did adults teach this concept to their children, but children perpetuated it among one another. The reality of this "generation curse," was quite evident as I sat among my peers, hearing their derisions.

Stella could have passed the brown paper bag test; she was medium-complexioned with beautiful hazel eyes. Stella blasted out, "you are black and you know your place, to the back," threw her head back and roared in laughter with the rest of the students. I was embarrassed. Soon after that episode the judges returned to the auditioning room. Nothing was said to the finalists as to the reason for their meeting. Miss Williams instructed me that she would begin to read, and at the right time I was to respond when I heard my cue. Fortunately for me, she began to read from the portion of script that I had committed to memory. Under what I perceived as a lot of pressure, the audition for the speaking part for Alice went off without a hitch.

When my audition was completed, the judges retired to a separate room to tally their votes. When the panel of judges reconvened in the classroom, the first face I noticed was Mr. Dorest, smiling with all thirty-two of his pearly whites. Mr. Simon, announced who had been selected to play each role, and thanked all of the students that had auditioned, assuring them of the great job each had done.

He paused in his lengthy discourse and explained that all of the participants were excellent in the competition for the part of Alice. He further explained that the decision was extremely difficult to make, in light of the fact that none of the competitors knew any of the singing parts. He went on to say that there was a mix up in communication between the annex and main campus, as to what criteria the participants would be judged by. By this time everyone was on the edge of their seats, and wanted him to get to the point immediately. Apparently, Mr. Simon, perceived our thoughts, and announced, "We have selected Pansy Bradshaw to play the leading role of Alice in our annual school play."

There was loud applause, and loud moans of disappointment. Mr. Dorest and Miss Jones were elated. They ran over to me and embraced me in their arms, telling me what a wonderful job I had done, and how proud they were that I had landed the leading character role.

Wondering whether I had heard correctly, it took me a while before the realization settled in that I had been selected to play the leading role of Alice. Finally, the actuality of the decision landed in my intelligence. I too became overjoyed and caught up in the excitement of the moment. I grabbed Mr. Dorest's and Miss Jones's hand and we literally skipped and kicked our legs in a jubilant victory dance. As we whirled around the room I caught Stella's eyes peering at me from across the room and I poked my tongue out at her.

Auditioning announcements continued, but I was caught up in being happy, really savoring the reality of what had happened. Dazed and full of joy as the announcements proceeded, I remained in this utopian state of mind. That day I could not tell anyone who was selected to play any other character, except Alice.

Auditioning being completed, we were instructed to hurry outside so that we would not miss the school bus. In my euphoric state of mind, I did not translate that directive as you will have to walk home. I stayed longer than I should have receiving compliments and congratulatory hugs from my peers and the teaching staff, thus missing the last school bus, and having to walk home from school. As I started my walk home I felt as though I was literally floating on a cloud which would zip me home in a flash. I was so caught up in joy and anxious to share all of the details of my being selected over all the other candidates. I could imagine myself sharing with my parents and sisters the wonderful victory at school. I imagined dramatizing the entire scenario with a spellbinding monologue.

Suddenly, I was jarred from my reverie by the blaring loud persistent honking of an automobile horn. Then I heard voices blasting as loud as the horn, such horrible words as, "NIGGER, BLACK SAMBO, TAR BABY, PICANINNY, STUPID UGLY NIGGER!!!" To my horror there was a car full of white teenage boys. The car was a white Ford, I remember seeing the Ford insignia. The driver parked the car on top of the viaduct. Clearly, I recall the driver of the automobile sitting behind the wheel yelling, as the other four occupants yelled out of the window at me. Constantly they taunted me to come closer to the car.

Totally frozen by fear, I watched as two white pimply faced teenage boys got out of the car and approached me. One of them had dark brown hair, and the other had blond hair. As they approached me, the three boys remaining in the car cried out to their friends, "KILL THAT BLACK NIGGER!" I was no match for these guys, the blond one was tall and lanky while the brown one was thick and muscular. I began to cry, rembling with fear the outcome of the ugly scene unfolded before my eyes. They began to push me around between the two of them one pushing me towards another, and the other pushing me toward his companion.

In an attempt to block out what was happening to me, I went someplace in my mind. I reflected on how warm the breezes were as they blew against my tear-streaked face. I could smell Nanny's freshly baked biscuits. I relived the visits to Audubon Park Zoo. The times my Mother would lovingly retrieve me from the bus that transported me home from nursery school.

The reality of what I was experiencing broke my protective mental barrier. Derogatory name calling, pushing, slapping and hitting in the face, on my head, and on my back with their fists, persisted. My dress was torn at the waist as I made an attempt to get out of their abusive physical attack. One of the white guys picked up a dirty, smelly burlap sack from the street curb, and began to beat me on my head and face with it. Burlap sacks were used to transport large amounts of crayfish, oysters in the shell, potatoes, or other vegetables.

The two other white boys were hanging out the door and windows of the car, laughing, encouraging their associates yelling, "Kick that nigger's a..! Kill her, kill her!" They pushed me so hard that I fell to my knees. As the kicking, pushing, and spitting continued, I crouched in a tucked position to protect my face and head from further attack.

Suddenly, a black car appeared on the overpass and it was filled with colored people. A middle aged couple, and their three teenage sons were in the car. They stopped the car, shouting, "LEAVE THAT CHILD ALONE!" The colored man and his sons were holding tire jacks, sticks, and a baseball bat. They yelled at my attackers, "STOP!" Hurriedly my white attackers ran to their car, jumped in and sped off.

The man and his wife shouted curse words at my assailants. "We will kick you're a ... for messing with our children, you were real bad attacking this one child. Come back now, while the odds are more even, you coward white bastards!" They countered back with the same type of horrible words that I had been subjected to, NIGGERS, TAR BABIES!! KISS OUR WHITE A. YOU BLACK SON OF A BITCH!!"

Carefully, the man and his wife picked me from the ground, collected my notebook and books, and placed me in their car. My rescuer's wife wiped my face and legs with her handkerchief, while constantly asking me was I all right? The man driving continuously screamed a flow of obscenity, confirming his hatred for whites. Their sons, who sat in the back seat of the auto were instructed by their Dad to always keep some type of stick, brick, bumper jack, to protect them-selves if they were ever accosted. Their father said, "I knew there would be a need for that bumper jack other than changing tires!" Basically, throughout my ride home with these kind people, I remained silent. They were outraged and still cursing at my white attackers.

The lady, who introduced herself as Miss Helen, asked me if I was hurting, did I feel the need to be taken to the hospital? As I shook my head no, I thought, all I want right now is to go home. Miss Helen offered to call my parents on the telephone and explain to them what she and her husband observed. Finally I broke my silence and told them, "Thank you very much but my parents are still at work and soon as they arrive home I will tell them what happened."

Miss Helen, concerned about my well-being and safety, asked me again "Are you sure you don't need medical attention?" Shaking my head no, I gave Miss Helen's husband my home address. I snuggled real close to Miss Helen for the remainder of the ride home. Finally, we arrived. I mumbled thanks and ran inside. Mae, as usual, was on the telephone Pat was playing in the back yard with our neighbors. Mother was not due home until 5:30, and Daddy normally got home between 10 and 10:30 PM. I was able to go into the bathroom, wash my face, and change clothing without my siblings' knowledge of the brutal attack.

At dinner that night, I shared the wonderful news of being selected to play the main character Alice, purposely I did not portray, nor dramatize all of the events that led up to my being selected. Nor did I share with any of them my devastating experience afterwards. In my immature evaluation, what could be done about it? Or, a better conclusion was, what would be done about it? I further rationalized if Mother or Daddy reported the incident to the all-white police department, would that action on their part subject our family to more racist attacks? Perhaps part of my reasoning for not telling my parents about the incident was that I was still adversely affected by the racial attack on me, and figured if I didn't discuss it with anyone, it would go away.

The play "Alice in Wonderland" went off without difficulty. At the final curtain call I was presented with a beautiful bouquet, three dozen of long-stemmed red roses. The audience clapped and clapped. We answered several curtain calls, and the audience even cried out "encore, encore," to the chorale final. Even though the play was a tremendous success, the adverse effect of the racial attack hovered in the back of my mind, prohibiting me from fully enjoying all of the enthusiasm and excitement. It was as if the residual affect was still indelibly etched in my mind creating a phobia, and an abhorrence, and low tolerance for anything or anybody that sanctioned racism.

Unfortunately, this vicious racial attack seemed to open a pathway for me to be sprayed with many other poisonous perfumes that scented my life.

PART TWO

POISONOUS PERFUMES

**Dead flies putrefy the perfumer's ointment, And
cause it to give off a foul odor. Ecclesiastics 10:1a NKJV**

In The Home

As I visually scanned my apartment, I thought I would make one more round to see if my auto keys, purse, or eye-glasses had been left behind. As I approached my room, my eyes moved toward the dresser, where several fragrances were showcased on the ornate, mirrored perfume tray. Keeping an eye on the fragrance I enjoy wearing the most, I thought, I'll get just one more spray of perfume. Walking out the door, I was thinking, how good the fragrance smelled. Making sure the door to my apartment was locked, and proceeding to the car, I mused I have probably overdosed on my favorite fragrance.

Enroute to the District Attorney's Office, where I was employed as a Family Support Officer, I thought on how many of life's experiences appeal to our olfactory senses. (seeing, hearing, smelling, tasting senses) that are deceptive. I remember Mother cautioning me about too much sugar is not good for you. She often warned me, " A moment on the lips, a lifetime on the hips!" "All that glitters is not gold!" "Everything that looks good to you is not good for you!" Was it possible that this good smelling perfume could be detrimental to my health?

I recall reading a magazine article about the chemicals used in creating colognes and perfumes are synthetic compounds derived from petroleum. Petroleum is capable of causing cancer, birth defects, central nervous disorders, allergic reactions, headaches, and asthma. The statistics are shocking and sobering. Is it possible that I was making myself sick with products, strategically placed on the consumer market, that appealed to my senses, but were harmful to my health and well being?

As I drove, I pondered human relationships and life's challenges. Those we chose and those that are thrust on us, when there is no choice made on our parts. Those things and persons that appeal to our senses, look good, feel good, smell good, taste good, in the passing of time can prove to be poisonous and detrimental to our health and well-being. I remembered more of the old adages, "Looks are deceiving!" The refrain, "Beauty is only skin deep!" That song reminded us to look farther than external appearances. Consequently, our natural senses can mislead us.

I reflected on how I met my husband, and how that man made a significant impact on all my senses. After Sunday School and eleven o'clock midday services, my sister Pat and I headed for the door. We were greeted by the Pastor, Rev. A. Monday, Rev. Monday was the Pastor of the St. Stephen Baptist Church. He was a short, bald headed, kind man that wore Coca Cola bottle thick eyeglasses. His interest in the youths went above and beyond the call of duty. He visited our instructors at school, asking about our behavior, grades and attitudes. These conferences with our instructors usually became a part of his Sunday Sermons, as he urged our parents to participate in the education of their children, as well as challenging us to excellence in behavior, superior scholastic achievements, and changes in our viewpoint on life. He had a way of asking us questions, and answering them with an affirmative. He would say, "I want to know where you children are going, and what are you doing now, yeah?" He was consistently repetitive in his conversations as well as in his sermon delivery.

Gwenie and I had taught and participated in Vacation Bible School, and had observed his mannerisms in speech, and we were both able to mimic him to perfection. Gwenie had a fine soprano voice that the director of the youth choir used often to lead hymns and sing solos. Even though I was older than Gwenie, and a couple of years ahead of her in school we shared a lot in common. We both sang at school functions, we lived in the same neighborhood, we both attended the LB Landry High School and St. Stephen Missionary Baptist Church.

Gwenie was a beautiful full-figured girl, with a full head of long black hair. Jenny was our friend, in school as well as at the church. Jenny, and Pat's boyfriend Jimmy, were related to each other. Even in her teenage years, Jenny was known to be an administrator. Jenny was the person to see at church if you wanted the job done right.

We all lingered at church, talking, and laughing. They were laughing about my wobbly walking in the highest heel shoes I had ever worn. I was experiencing the task of steadily walking on what felt like stilts. I had just turned sixteen years old, and Mother permitted me to purchase my first pair of spike heeled shoes.

Meeting My Husband

As we stood around the church, preparing for the walk home, Pat's boyfriend Jimmy, drove up in a 1953 green '98 Oldsmobile. As he got out of the car, the other front door opened also, and out stepped this gorgeous, six foot US Navy man dressed in full uniform whites, with the bell bottomed pant legs! My knees became weak, my stomach churned, my goodness, I thought this is about the best-looking man that I had seen in my life! I was immediately smitten. This man had a smooth cocoa brown complexion, wavy black hair, long curly eyelashes, with thick black eyebrows, and a cute mustache trimmed neatly over his top lip.

Gwenie and Jenny—normal teenagers—swooned. Normally, whenever good-looking boy came into our presence, we'd all begin to giggle and flutter our eyelashes, giving flirtatious looks to the guys. But this time, even though my girlfriends acted out, I stood firm and did not join in. I stood still until Jimmy and this "hunk" got out of the car.

When Jimmy approached where we were standing, he introduced us to his friend, Larry. Gwenie and Jenny were still giggling and batting their eyes in flirtatious approval, said "Hi my name is Jenny," Gwenie responded in an unnatural deep resonant voice, "my name is Gwenie." While extending my hand, with my most engaging smile, I said "My name is Pansy."

Later on, Larry told us his real name was Larry Ramon, and he was from St. Louis, Missouri. Jimmy, Pat's boyfriend, asked us where were we headed to, our response was, home. Jimmy suggested that we take a ride to the US Naval Base, to eat some ice cream. Pat and I both declined. We had not asked prior permission from Mother and she was expecting us home after church. Jimmy, then offered to give us a ride around the corner to our home. We accepted, told our giggly friends, Gwenie and Jenny, goodbye and got in the car. Pat jumped in the front seat with Jimmy, and sat snuggled up to him. Without careful observation, one could not tell who was driving, Pat or Jimmy.

During our short drive home, Larry asked "How are you classified?" My response was, "I am in my last year of high school." He told me he had just gotten out of boot camp, and he would be stationed at the Naval Base for several months, before shipping out to San Diego, Ca. When we arrived at the front of our house, I told Larry it was my pleasure to meet him. Before I got out of the car, he said, "Well, wait a minute, will I be able to see you again? What is your telephone number? Is it all right with your parents for me to call you sometime?" My mind thought, don't pinch me, this is a dream, and I do not want to wake up! Totally taken aback by this attention I was getting, and completely taken off my feet that Larry asked me for my phone number. I fumbled with the handle of the car, and tried to make a smooth exit. I mumbled our telephone number to Larry, in an endeavor to keep a cool mature demeanor. I could not believe my ears! Has he really asked to come and see me? Will this courtship end in marriage? It was customary for a young man, desiring to court a young lady, to ask her parent's permission. Larry had to overcome that hurdle, but I felt that if he was interested, he would not mind adhering to Southern tradition and formalities.

My experience having a man or boy show me attention was limited to my Daddy. My encounters with boys were limited to whistles, compliments, and aggravation. Whistles, because at sixteen years old my body had developed; and even though Mother did not permit us to wear revealing tight clothing, the development of my body was apparent. Compliments due to my singing talent resulted in my being appointed to sing our daily devotional on the public address system every morning. I also always landed a leading role in the annual musical drama. Aggravated, because prior to my becoming a developed teenager, I was a female fighter, a tomgirl.

During those formative years, I out fought, outtalked, and was basically quite competitive with boys. Scholastically, my grades began to take a nose dive as my interest in boys increased. It was not that I could not do the work assigned, nor was it that I did not fully comprehend the assignment. Call it an hormonal imbalance, distraction, lack of motivation, spring fever, or just plain growing up. But here I as, chronologically a child, physically having natural attractions for the opposite sex. Distracted because my aggressive, competitive relationship with boys had changed and I did not know how to make a smooth transition. I had no motivation to be aggressive to tell any boy that I liked him, because of the stigma of being identified as one of the "fast" girls. Fast girls were those girls that relentlessly pursued boys, hat allowed boys to go all the way with them. They drank alcoholic beverages, had illegal abortions, and went to the clubs and bars.

During the times in which I was reared, a common practice observed by most African American families was that you were considered grown when you were either twenty one years of age, or living independently from your parents, whichever came first. Then came the Vietnam war when young men eighteen years old were being drafted into the military to fight for their country. This concept of being grown at the age of twenty one years old was challenged by Vietnam war dissidents. Their concept was that if I am old enough to fight, and possibly die for my country, then I am grown at eighteen years old, and can vote, buy alcoholic beverages, and tobacco products and be permitted entry into night clubs. At eighteen years old, one should be independent from parental consultation, freed from the former traditions and legal constraints.

This liberal way of life was not the case in my rearing. We had to be subject to our parents. In order to court me, Larry had to speak with my Dad and make his intentions known. So

Larry told my parents that he liked me, and wanted to begin courting me to see if there was a possibility of us furthering our relationship in marriage. This old-fashioned way sounds almost like a modern pre-nuptial agreement—your intentions were made clear to the girl's parents prior to you starting to see her on a regular basis.

When we got in the house, Mother's inquiry was who was sitting in the back seat with me? I told her that his name was Larry, he was in the US Navy, stationed at the Naval Station. She then asked, "How old is he?"

"About twenty or twenty–one years old."

"I think he is too matured for you."

"Mother I caught a ride home from church with Jimmy, and Larry was in the car. However, he did ask if it was all right with you and Daddy that he can call me and talk with me on the telephone."

"Your Daddy and I will have to talk this over, we do not know this young man, nor do we know anything about his people."

My thoughts began to wander to my sisters and their boy-friends experiences with my parents. I realized even at sixteen years old that this was their way of protecting us. However, I really wanted them to not be quite so rigid and grant me permission to talk on the telephone with Larry.

Mae's boyfriend went through the same scrutiny, if not worse. I recall one night in particular that Bill and Mae were courting, and Daddy arrived home from work around 10:30 PM. Bill and Mae were still listening to the radio and phono-graph when he arrived. He bided them good evening, and proceeded to his room. I do not know whether Dad was provoked at work, or whether Mother had encouraged this confrontation. After his bath, he put on his pajamas and robe, and came to the living room where Bill and Mae were still sitting at around 11:00 P.M. He asked Bill. "What are your intentions?" Bill said, " I don't know what you mean." Daddy replied, " For the last three months, every weekend night when I arrive home you are here, and I want to know what are your intentions?" "Do you plan on marrying my daughter?" "If not, why are you wasting her time?"

Pat and I, hearing the entire conversation, began to snicker and comment on Mae's obvious embarrassment. Little did we know that in not too many years to come we would have to deal with the same scenario—different time, different people, but the same tradition scrutiny, and formalism.

Anxiously I waited for Larry to call, and Mother and Daddy to give me their decision as to whether or not it was all right to receive telephone calls from Larry. About three weeks from the Sunday I met Larry, Mother called me into the kitchen and said, "Your Daddy and I have talked and we are of the opinion that we would rather you not involve yourself with this Navy man. Your grades are already going down, and we feel that any other involvement on your part would only lead to your grades declining further. In addition we have no information about this young man nor his family."

My heart dropped, I felt very angry, and too sheltered. How could my parents get to know him if they did not open the door for him to become familiar with them? I felt that my parents were being unreasonably unfair. However, she continued, " We have decided that we will allow you to accept telephone calls from Larry on weekends only." I threw my arms around my Mother's neck, kissing her all over her face and saying, "Thank you, thank you, thank you, I love you, I love Daddy too!" Mother gave me one stipulation, they expected my grades to improve or the telephone conversations would cease.

Still very excited about their decision, I hurriedly agreed to restore my grades back to the B average level. Happily I skipped to my room to share the news with Pat. She told me, "I already knew, I heard Mother and Daddy discussing it this morning before Dad left for work." She said that she had called Jimmy, and told him of our parents decision. He would make sure Larry knew it was all right to call. Floating on air I hugged Pat and told her that she was my very best friend and I loved her much.

Eagerly, I waited for the telephone to ring. I wanted to hear one of my sisters tell me that Larry was on the telephone. If Larry made an attempt to get through on the phone he would have been greeted with a busy signal, for Pat and Jimmy stayed on the telephone for an unprecedented record of two hours. When I complained to Mother she merely smiled very tolerantly and said, "Jimmy doesn't call often." I went to bed disappointed because Pat stayed on the telephone with her boyfriend so long. She was fully aware that after a certain time Larry was not permitted to make telephone calls, nor could I receive telephone calls after 9:30 PM. As I drifted off to sleep, my thoughts wandered, Will I ever be able to talk with Larry? I knew that he was attracted to me, and certainly I was head over heels infatuated with him. Why was fate keeping us apart?

As an inexperienced sixteen year old teenager, I blamed my parents, my sisters, the Navy, and anything and anybody else that materialized in my mind that hindered us from talking. Frustrated with my circumstances, I fell off to sleep.

Finally, on the following night, just as I finished washing dinner dishes, the phone rang. Mother answered it and jokingly whispered to me, "It is Prince Larry!" Hurriedly, I dried my hands, retrieved the phone from Mother and retired to my room, to talk with Larry without interfering ears listening to my conversation. My sisters and my Mother would want to listen to every word, so to prevent the expected I locked the door.

As time progressed and the holiday season came, I was quite pleased and surprised that on Thanksgiving Day, Larry gave me a friendship ring. In my eyes this fourteen karat ring held three of the largest diamonds, I had ever seen. In reality these diamonds were diamond chips. Because I was looking through the eyes of love, it really did not matter what the size or cost was. When I accepted Larry's friendship ring, we decided that it was time for him to ask my Mom and Dad for the privilege of courting me. We did ask and surprisingly there were no long sermons, regarding his intentions and whether or not they were honorable, nor was there a long discourse about Larry being much more mature than I, or his being a Navy man. Only permission to court me was granted. I was pleasantly surprised that Larry was not subjected to the type of interrogation I'd heard my sister's boyfriends receive. We were thrilled that Larry was given consent to keep courting me.

Every weekend Larry was allowed to visit our home to keep company with me. Keeping company involved listening to records, watching television, kissing and hugging when an opportunity to be alone presented itself. Larry had my parent's consent to escort me to school functions, basketball and football games, and record hops. I felt so special whenever he would escort me to school functions. Both girls and boys were jealous when they saw us—the guys because they resented a stranger, especially a Navy man dating one of their girls, and the girls because Larry was so good looking. They thought, "What does he see in her?" I knew that this good looking, good smelling, good talking, good gift giving man was for me! As my grades improved, so did my fondness for Larry.

Mother and Daddy became more liberal allowing Larry to escort me to church, the US Naval Base, just to eat ice cream sundaes, to go bowling, play Ping-Pong, and my personal favorite, to play the pin ball machine.

Mother and Daddy began to counsel me more than usual about preparing for a future in college, but I had other plans. My plans included becoming Larry's wife, and traveling all over the world with him, and raising a family. In my senior year of high school, while the rest of my peers were preparing to live away from home on college campuses, or enlist in the military, or enter the job market, my plans for the future, were " to be Larry's wife till death do us part".

In November of 1959 Larry got orders. He was to be reassigned from New Orleans to the US Lexington that was docked in San Diego, California. I was broken hearted! Larry was to report for duty by June 1960. This disheartening news could not have come at a worse time. In May of 1960, I would celebrate my 17th birthday, I had the leading role in a musical drama entitled, "The Fortune Teller and, I was to graduate from high school in June. All of the graduating class of L. B. Landry High School was scheduled for several written examinations, to determine if we would actually graduate from high school, and finally this news.

From the time that Larry shared with me that he was to ship out to San Diego, I was depressed. A dark, dismal depression took over me. My academic scores suffered, my sleep was troubled. In two months I lost fifteen pounds. My whole world had been turned upside down due to what I considered, in my love struck state of mind to be a plot initiated by the US Government, and the US Navy, to keep Larry and me apart. As absurd as this thought was, it was all too real for me.

My usual Christmas spirit of decorating the house, baking cookies, cakes, pies, making candy, going Christmas shopping, exchanging gifts, visiting each of our friends homes, no longer carried the excitement, thrill or stimulation that I once loved so much. My thoughts were consumed with negative reasoning. Larry will find someone else, we will never see each other again in this life! All I'll have to remember him is this friendship ring and my memories. I had no alternate plans for my life. My life, as I thought, ceased without Larry. I was miserable. Mother and Daddy were concerned about me not eating. Mother became so concerned she figured a trip to our family doctor, Dr. Golden was necessary.

Dr. Golden, was Mother's gynecologist for many years, and when my sisters and I were old enough to see a female specialist, he was the obvious choice. He was a short, white haired Jewish man, who was very personable and concerned about Mose and Mary's offsprings. He always questioned us about our grades were, which college were we planning on attending, and if we had considered the medical field? Perhaps he asked because he desired to help with tuition or admission if our answers were yes, maybe it was just his normal bedside mannerisms, but it was very nice of him to ask.

This visit, Mother voiced her concerns about my weight loss and my loss of appetite. Dr. Golden performed a thorough physical examination including specimen for further lab test. During the exam he asked the usual questions, "how are your grades, what university are you planning on attending?" My response was, "My grades have declined lately." He then asked, "why"? I explained to him that I had met this absolutely great guy, and with my parent's permission, we began to date. Giving him the entire scenario, I concluded by sharing with Dr. Golden that my boyfriend had received orders to be stationed in San Diego, California, and I was feeling pretty low because I felt that we would never see each other again in life. He smiled, and said, " How sweet is young love!" He then told me that he felt I was too young to be all depressed about a situation that obviously I had no control over. He added, "Pansy, you have your entire future ahead of you, don't get hung up in adult relationships before time." Well I was absolutely frustrated with his advice. My thoughts were, you have no idea of what I am going through, and you tell me to not enter into an adult relationship, and my heart is already totally involved.

Dr. Golden reported to Mother that based upon his findings in the physical exam I was healthy and whole. He also informed her that he sent my blood and urine specimens to the laboratory, and would report to her if the there were any adverse findings.

Blues On Christmas

By Christmas Day of 1959, as we sat to dinner with the entire family, I was still drooping around the house. Mother, as usual had prepared a sumptuous meal that consisted of roasted turkey, baked ham, prime ribs, gumbo, mixed vegetables, collard greens, potato salad, dirty rice, green salad, succotash, brown gravy, cornbread dressing, cranberry sauce, apple pie, pecan pie, pound cake, homemade ice cream, and various types of sodas for our non-alcoholic drinking guests. It was customary in our neighborhood for the adults to visit each other's home, drinking alcohol and getting to know one another in a more intimate social setting.

Larry was invited to our home for Christmas dinner. To further the disappointment I was experiencing, Larry did not arrive at the house to eat dinner with the family as scheduled. After eating Christmas dinner with my family, I excused myself and went to my room to sulk. We finished eating and cleaning up the dishes at about 3:30 PM. Four thirty, five thirty, passed as I heard every second that the clock ticked off. By six thirty, I just knew he would not come. My mind went astray with thinking contrary illusions. During those three hours I had recurring bouts of crying and sleeping. My entire family knew that I was disappointed that Larry had not showed up for dinner, and they honored my desire to be alone in my room.

My Mother finally broke the silence as she knocked at the door. "Pansy," she called out, "May I come in?" I answered, "come in." She sat on the side of my bed, and said Most of our guests' are wondering if you are feeling well." I told my Mother, "I don't feel much like being an entertaining hostess, Mother would you please tell them something for me?" She said, "no, normally you are the life of the party and you've been in here drooping around too long, wash your face and

reapply your make up, and come and join the other guests."
Reluctantly, I complied with her request, and joined the family
members and guests in the living room and kitchen. As I
approached the living room, I smelled a familiar, distinctive
fragrance. It smelled like Aqua Velva men's cologne, the very
fragrance that Larry wore.

As I walked to the living area, I was warmly greeted by
the family and neighbors that I had excused myself from about
three and one half hours ago. Mother asked me would I please
see to it that the guests' drinks were refilled, and to replenish
their desserts if they so desired. I went to the kitchen to get ice
and to freshen the drinks, when suddenly I heard "BOO!"
Startled, I jumped and Larry came from behind the door.
Squealing with delight I hugged his neck and kissed him. From
the living room I heard Mother's voice say, "She is back from
the dead because her prince has arrived." Bursts of laughter
came from the living room. We were too involved with each
other to care if we were the object of their jokes.

In between kisses and hugs I asked, "Where have you
been?" "Why didn't you call me?" Larry put his fingers to my
mouth, hushing me, and said, "I'll answer all your questions,
but right now I have some questions to ask you." I thought, I
was the one who should be asking questions. You have disappointed and embarrassed me in front of my family and friends!

Larry put his hand in his pocket and pulled out a purple
velvet ring box. My heart began to race. He looked me
squarely in the eyes and said, "Pansy, I am in love with you,
and since I will have to leave New Orleans to be stationed in
San Diego, I do not desire to be without you for the rest of my
life. Will you be my wife? Will you marry me before I leave
for San Diego?" Flabbergasted, amazed, and thrilled, I cried.
As tears of joy streamed down my face, somewhere in the
midst of the overwhelming emotions, I responded, "YES!"
Larry took my hand and placed my diamond engagement ring
on my left hand, third finger. He then showed me the matching

diamond-encrusted wedding band. Totally engulfed by my euphoric state of mind, I continued to hug him and kiss him, telling him, "I'll be delighted to be your wife!"

Quickly Larry walked me into the living room where the rest of the family and friends were sitting. He yelled out loud, "I have something to share with you. Mr. & Mrs. Bradshaw, I have asked Pansy to marry me before I leave for San Diego in June. She has consented, to be my wife and we'd like to receive your blessings." Mother and Daddy looked at Larry and I, then at each other as Daddy said, "you are both so young, and Pansy has led a sheltered life. Nevertheless, we give you our blessings and approval." Smiling, Larry grabbed me into his arms and shouted to the room," I love Pansy, and she is going to be my wife yippee!" Needless to say, I was so excited that Larry asked me to marry him and that my parents had given their approval and blessings. I was walking around the rest of the evening on cloud nine. This is what I had been hoping and praying, that we would spend our lives together.

I could not wait to get to school when the holidays were over to show off my engagement ring. I wanted to see the envious stares on some of my classmates' faces, as they looked at the ring, and knew that they had not located their "Prince" yet, and they did not have any prospects. In my excited state of mind I was still thinking ahead. What kind of wedding should I have? Formal or informal? Morning or afternoon? How many bride and groom attendants? How many guests? Where would the reception be? What types of food and drinks would be served? Where would we spend our honeymoon? Invitations or word of mouth?

Larry told me that he was delayed for Christmas dinner because his parents had driven unexpectedly from Meridian, Mississippi to Christmas dinner with him. He explained, "My Mom and Dad already know about you, and have seen the rings that I purchased for you. I told them that it would be all right for them to accompany me to your parents' house but they opted to get back on the road before it was too late." Larry told me his parents were looking forward to meeting me, but felt they would unfairly intrude in that it was a major holiday, and they were not expected nor invited guests.

Later on I found out that the reason Daddy and Mother had given a quick consent to such a young marriage. They were afraid that if they did not give consent, I would do something foolish, like running away or becoming pregnant. Needless to say I never thought of such a thing; however, I would have been greatly devastated and disappointed if my parents decided to oppose our marriage.

In my busy schedule—in addition to the opera performance, "The Fortune Teller," high school graduation, class night, prom—I had to plan, my wedding. I was happy the way my life was going. I tackled each event as it presented itself with the very utmost of assurance, and care, and following each one to completion.

The largest and most complex task was coordinating, and planning, my wedding and reception. Mother, Larry and I sat for hours figuring out a way for us to have a nice wedding and reception, at the most economical cost, without compromising quality or quantity. Larry was permitted by the Naval Station Officer's Club to book the facility at no charge because he was in the military. Painstakingly we slimmed the guest roster down to three hundred fifty.

Traditionally it was the responsibility of the bride's parents to purchases all of the food and drinks, the photographer, the Ministerial honorarium, floral bouquets for the bride, and bridesmaids, and lapel corsages for the groomsmen, and the limousine and other cars participating in the motorcade. Larry agreed to the expenses for the wedding cake, invitations, thank you cards, gifts for the bridesmaids and groomsmen, floral decorations for the church and the banquet room at the Naval Station.

When the day of my wedding finally arrived, I was absolutely exhausted. Mother, with her innovative homemade remedies, put a solution of witch hazel, mint leaves, and cold cream on a towel, and then put it on my face. It was a wonderfully exhilarating experience, and temporarily the mixture removed dark circles from under my fatigued eyes, and gave my skin a beautiful ebony glow.

My wedding dress was borrowed from Carol, my cousin. She had gotten married two years before me and she and my Mother decided that, with a few alterations, the dress would fit me perfectly. This decision saved my parents several hundred dollars that could be used for other things.

The wedding gown was a beautiful white embroidered organza dress with long pointed sleeves. It had a princess fitted top that flowed into a heavily gathered full floor length skirt, with an attached eight-foot train. The floor length gathered skirt, sleeves, and train were seeded with white pearls. The matching veil of illusion was also seeded with pearls. The tiara that the veil was attached to was also made of pearls. My shoes were embroidered white patent leather, opened on both sides of the shoe at the arch, with enclosed toe and heel. My bridesmaids were dressed in multiple pastel shades of pink, yellow, green, and blue of the same organza material without the embroidery, with coordinating color headpieces and dyed color-coordinated satin pumps.

Larry's groomsmen wore white dinner jackets and black tuxedo formal pants, while the groom was clothed, in an all-white formal tuxedo. The day before the wedding, my girlfriends; Joyce and Gloria; and my sister Pat, with Althea all went to the church to decorate the pews, the arch, and the aisle leading to the altar. Even though we had no prior decorating experience, we did and admirable job with the decorating project. Pew markers were made of crepe paper. Artistically perfect white, pink, yellow, and green bunches of gladiolas with coordinating streamers marked every third pew.

Meticulously, we laid the white runner that stretched from the front door of the church, down the middle aisle, all the way to the altar. We would stand under an arch, decorated with white crepe paper doves and rosebuds, and kneel to be prayed for on a white kneeler decorated with the same white crepe paper doves and rose buds with white satin ribbon streamers.

Mother wore a simple pink raw silk dress with pink pearl jewelry and dyed pink satin shoes. Daddy had on a white dinner jacket and black formal trousers.

My Wedding Day

On the day of the wedding, Mother and Daddy arose around four AM to start cleaning the house and preparing the food for the wedding guests. Daddy had our patio furniture loaded down with chicken, turkey, ham, and tuna salad sandwiches. There were numerous trays of fried chicken, fried fish, potato salad, cakes, pies, green salads, dips, chips, pickles, dishes of dinner mints, and large crocks of homemade lemonade, punch, cases of beer, carbonated drinks, and cases of bourbon, gin, vodka, and rum. Pots of gumbo, dirty rice, collard greens, and candied sweet potatoes, and corn bread were customarily served at the bride's home, where family, close friends and those that helped to serve at the reception, would gather after the reception had ended.

Larry's parents arrived a couple of hours, before the ceremony. They drove from Meridian, Mississippi, and did not go to the base because there was no place for Larry to accommodate them. So it was pre-arranged that they would stop at my parents' house. In the midst of all the activity and anxiety, I was given the task of introducing myself to my soon-to-be in-laws, and seeing to it that they were comfortable, introducing them to the rest of the family and friends, offering them food, a place to change clothing, or rest. "Hi, I'm Pansy," I said in the most charming, hospitable manner that I possessed. Larry's dad extended his hand and said, "We have heard many positive things about you from our son, and we are looking forward to you spending time in Mississippi, with the rest of our family, before you leave to join Larry in San Diego." I was completely fascinated by this ebony complexioned man with gray sideburns. He was quite stately, and an extremely good looking older man. I mumbled, " It is my pleasure to meet you." Amazed at how strikingly good looking this man was, I pondered, is this what Larry will look like when he is older? Larry's dad was about six feet three inches tall, with graying sideburns that framed his chocolate face. His eyes were very dreamy looking with long silky black eye-lashes, and the most beautiful set of pearly white teeth that flashed when he smiled.

Turning my attention to Larry's mom, I extended my hand to her, which she did not take. She asked, "How did you guys ever talk Larry into marriage?" Larry's Mother was a very beautiful cafe au lait–complexion, hazel eyed woman with long black wavy hair that flowed almost to her waist. I learned later that her grandfather was a full blooded Creek Indian. Astounded, I looked at her with my mouth ajar. I did not know how to answer her. I felt there was a reason for her asking the question, but I choose to ignore her.

I invited Larry's parents to the bedroom to change clothes, to eat, or drink anything they desired. Larry's Dad accepted, his Mom said, "I prefer not to eat here!" Hurriedly, I directed them to the backyard, where Mother and Daddy were busy with last-minute food preparations and delivery to the Naval Station for the reception. "Mother and Daddy, meet Larry's parents. Ms. Helen and Mr. Raymond, Mose and Mary Bradshaw." Mr. Raymond shook both my parents hands. Ms. Helen, asked the same question she had asked me. "How in the world did you all talk Larry into getting married?" My Mother's left eyebrow went up! We all knew that this was a sign that Mother was quite perturbed; when she arched her left eyebrow, you were about to be told off in no uncertain terms.

"Sweetheart," she began, "what on earth would make you think someone had to force your son into marriage?" "When you married your husband did you or your family compel him to marry you?" Larry's Dad, in an attempt to make an embarrassing moment seem humorous, said, "Yeah Helen, did you force me into marriage?" "If I remember correctly you and I said we loved each other, and did not want to be without each other for the rest of our lives!" Mother responded, "I am sure that is what has happened with Larry and Pansy! However, if you really need verification of this, I suggest you ask your son."

With that statement Mother and Daddy returned to finishing the task of preparing the food. I thought, welcome to your new family, Pansy. I was so glad that my Mother had an appropriate answer, for what obviously was not a very kind thing to ask of your prospective daughter-in-law, nor her parents.

Subsequently, I learned the reason that Larry's Mom asked that question was because, she immediately associated us with the dark side of New Orleans that practiced witchcraft. Her conclusion was that black magic had been practiced on her son in order to force him into a marriage.

Winding through the streets of New Orleans, the motorcade cruised with blaring automobile horns announcing that we had been married. Silently, and happily I lay in Larry's arms as the driver of the limousine followed a pre - planned route. We both began to reflect on the wedding ceremony, and how every detail was picture perfect, as though we were afforded a perfect day for the perfect match! I thought in my mind, what a storybook day, we had temperatures in the low 80's, normally temps soared above 95-98 degrees with humidity that made it almost impossible to breathe.

The church was packed inside with invited guests, outside were spectators, and well-wishers wanting to get a look at the bride, bridegroom, and the attendees. While outside sitting in the car, I could hear the organ music and see the processional as they began their trek down the center aisle of the church. As the little flower girls began to enter, I knew that this was my cue to prepare to get out of the car, and enter into the vestibule of the church. The music stopped for what seemed to me forever, and then the musicians began to play "The Wedding March." I positioned myself behind the entry door of the sanctuary, Daddy joined me, and kissed me, saying, "I wish the best for you in this new life you are undertaking, you are beautiful, and I love you so much." I had to restrain myself from crying and streaking my make up, but my eyes did well up with water. Composing myself as the church doors swung open, Daddy and I marched down the aisle, where Larry met us, Daddy took my hand, kissed me on the cheek again, then placed my hand into Larry's hand.

Brought back from my thoughts of a perfect day, for a perfect match, as we approached the gate of the US Naval Station in New Orleans. Larry showed his military identification, and informed the sentinel that there were approximately 50-70 cars that were all invited guests to our wedding reception. The guard came to attention, saluted us, and waved us through the gate. I was informed by some guests that each car that came through that gate was given in the same formal military salute making each guest feel very special.

This was the first time in the history of the US Naval Station that a wedding reception had been held on the base, and all the attendees were African Americans. Therefore the guests were very excited about being able to go and party on a military base. Party, we did! It is commonplace in New Orleans for revelry, merry making, and plenty of festivity to take place, at any given time—be it marriage, Tuesdays, death, birth of a child, or just because it is today. The wedding and reception were perfect. Everything went off without an obstacle.

Larry and I left the wedding reception early in order to travel a short distance to our hotel. Our one week stay would be our honeymoon. We had an excellent stay at the little hotel right outside of New Orleans. It was family owned and operated hotel, and the family made sure that we were provided with service and privacy. We swam, played miniature golf, but for the most of our time there we spent together in our room. After our honeymoon we returned to my Daddy and Mother's home to live with them until it was time for Larry to report to his new duty station aboard the USS Lexington.

During the day, we had the house to ourselves, due to Mother and Daddy's work schedule. It was my responsibility to cook for my new husband and to keep house. We spent a lot of time with my friends from the neighborhood. As we opened our wedding gifts, we were overjoyed to find out that most of our bedding and bath needs had already been supplied.

The gift that I most overjoyed about was this one bottle of champagne, and two crystal long-stemmed wine glasses. This gift had been given to us by one of my favorite instructors in high school, Miss Halthean. Miss Halthean, was the head of the Music Department at L. B. Landry High School. I made a lot over the gift, and thought a lot about that gift, and asked Larry did he mind if we didn't open it until, I arrived in San Diego? He said "Honey, I think that is a good idea, we can celebrate appropriately in our first apartment together." Neatly I tucked the bottle of champagne away in the bedroom closet towards the rear so that the bottle would not roll out accidentally and break.

One day I was returning home from grocery shopping, I entered the house and put the groceries on the kitchen table. I heard laughter from the backyard and went to the back window to investigate, I saw Larry and three of his groomsmen from the Naval base in the backyard laughing and basically having a good time. After putting the groceries away, I went out to greet the guys, and noticed a bottle of wine that resembled my gift, lying in the grass, with several bottles of beer. Not giving the empty bottle of wine much more though, I excused myself from Larry and his visitors to start to prepare dinner. Larry's guest did not stay long after I arrived back from the market.

Two Weeks After The Wedding

Larry walked his friends to the front and joined me in the kitchen. I asked Larry "Was that our special bottle of wine that I saw empty on the grass?" He said, "Yeah, and what about it?" I said, "I thought we had agreed to not drink that champagne until I arrived in San Diego?" Larry became very rude and belligerent, and told me to leave him alone. I continued to question him as to why he had not consulted with me, or gone to the store to buy himself and his friends something else to drink?

Suddenly, Larry arose from where he was seated, came over near me, raised his hand and slapped me full across my face! "Shut up," he yelled! Larry then balled up his fist, and punched me in my face! I screamed, and cried out "What are you hitting me for? I just wanted to know was this our special wine?" He yelled at me, as I cowered in the corner crying, "I am the man in this family, and whatever I say or do, I do not want to be questioned by you. You are never to ask me any questions as to what I do, or the reasons. I will exercise my headship in this family, do you understand me?"

Crying in the corner, I did not answer, my mind was wondering what had happened to provoke this response? He yelled at me again, "Do you hear me?" He then stooped down, and struck me in my head with his fists. Rolling over on my back, yelling in pain and crying, I said through tears of fear, shock, and disappointment, "Yeah, I hear you!" I was physically and emotionally in shock. In my mind I had not done nor said anything that justified this severe reaction. I thought to myself, my husband is crazy!

I got up off the floor ran to my room, locked myself in for the entire afternoon, until Mother and Daddy arrived home from work. Daddy got home from work about twenty minutes

63

before Mother. From down the hall I could hear Larry explaining to my Daddy that he did not know what was wrong with me, that I had locked myself in the bedroom since early afternoon.

I yelled from the protection of my barricaded bedroom "You are a liar, you know darn well what is wrong with me, you slapped me in my face and punched me in my head!" Daddy, yelled back, "Are you all right? Come out Daddy is home." My response was, "I'd rather tell this thing one time when Mother arrives home." I did not want to go over telling this horrible attack two times. From the protection of my barricaded bedroom, I could hear mumblings of Larry talking to Daddy. Lying on the bed crying as I waited for Mother to come home from work, I had to figure out why this happened.

Through my tears, I thought what a detestable way to treat one's wife of two weeks. Larry promised to love cherish and honor me until death parted us. It appeared to me from what I had experienced with Larry's brutal attack, that my death was imminent.

Unfortunately it only took me two weeks into marriage for me to begin to realize that all that smelled good, looked good, talked good, knew how to give good gifts was not good for me. This spray of perfume was undeservingly scathing, unexpectedly applied, and underminded the very foundation of our marriage. I was victimized by spousal abuse. A victim of domestic violence before domestic violence had its proper name.

When Mother arrived home, as soon as I heard her voice I ran from my room, blurting out the events that had just happened to me. Mother stood looking at me in disbelief, and Daddy was furious with Larry. The muffled voices that I could not discern while locked in my room crying, was Larry lying to my Daddy about what had really happened. Daddy told Larry, "Man you have got to be some kind of a fool, you are staying in my house, eating my food, and beating up my daughter!" Mother broke into the conversation and said, "We are peace loving people, but my husband and I will kick your narrow behind about beating our daughter. When we gave her to you as a wife, she came unharmed, and we don't expect you to treat her any different!" Larry became very belligerent and told my parents, "As far as your house and your daughter is concerned, I found her here and I can leave her here!" While Larry was retrieving his duffel bag from the closet, he yelled out to my parents and to me, "I am her husband and she is going to listen to me, because I am the man in this relationship! When she arrives in San Diego there will be no one there to help her!"

Larry left my parents' home and went to the Naval Base. Within three hours he had telephoned my parents apologizing to them, and requesting to speak with me. I was too hurt and distraught to talk to Larry or anyone else. Mother and Daddy made every attempt to console me by telling me that I could annul my marriage and go away to college. I was so terribly confused. I did not know what to think, what to do, or what course of action to take. I just wanted all of the things that I had experienced to go away. I did not accept any of Larry's telephone calls. I was angry and hurt. I walked around the house in bewilderment.

One day while Mother and Daddy were at work. I heard a knock at the front door. I yelled out. "Who is it?" "Pansy, it's me, Larry!" Frightened, I yelled out, "Go away or I will call the police!" Larry's voice came back in a softened tone, "just wanted to tell you that I will be leaving for San Diego on tomorrow, and I am so sorry about what I did to you. Please forgive me! I don't know what happened to me, I just lost it, please forgive me. I love you, I want you to spend the rest of my life with you."

Larry's voice began to crack and I could hear him crying. I was not moved by his request for forgiveness, or his crying. My response was, "Get away from me, you are a horrible person and I never want to see you anymore!" "Pansy, please" he pleaded! I mean it Larry I will call the police!" After a long silence from the other side of the door, I heard him say, "OK, I'll leave, but be expecting your allotment check in the mail within three months. If you are ill, your dependent's military ID should take you to any military hospital to be treated free of charge. I love you, and I hope to see you in San Diego!" When I heard the words San Diego, his words to me and my parents sprang back into my mind, "There will be no one to help you in San Diego!" How farsighted his words proved to be.

Relentlessly, Larry pursued me to join him in San Diego. It is amazing how time, youth, and love are excellent aids to forgiving and forgetting. Eventually, I gave in and reconciled with Larry. My parents were in opposition to our reconciliation, however they understood young love. When I left New Orleans, I left with confidence from my Mother and Daddy that if things got too bad, I was always welcome home.

Queen For The Day

Upon my arrival in San Diego, I was treated like a Queen. Larry was very attentive, loving and caring. We agreed that while he was stationed aboard the aircraft carrier, I should go to college. Little did we know that those plans would have to be canceled, due to my becoming pregnant with our son. Larry was an absolute perfect husband to me. For the first time in our marriage, I experienced the joy that I so longed for. But as the old saying goes, "All good things must come to an end!" Eventually the end of good times did come in the most unexpected manner. I recall the incident that brought the end of good times. Larry and I had been discussing our son's daycare. I was enrolled in college. Larry was not thrilled about my attending college. His position was that since he was the breadwinner, he should be enrolled in college. However, due to his work schedule in the Navy, his only option was to go to evening classes. Larry was of the opinion that the evening college classes took too long to complete the necessary amount of units required for graduation. Nevertheless, Larry consented to my attending day classes at the university.

In an attempt to mask his selfish desires, he came up with a complete reversal of the decision that we had made together. Larry's feigned concern for our son's care was his reason to prohibit me from attending college. All of my classes from Monday through Friday were completed by 11 AM each day. I was normally home before 11:30 each day. Day care for our son consisted of me taking our child out of his bed and placing him in the next door neighbor's bed prior to my leaving for class.

Fighting For My Life

Naturally the position that I took was not compatible with Larry's dictatorship policy. There was no provocation from me that sparked this attack. Just because I did not agree with his decision, Larry punched me in my face, then proceeded to slap and kick me continuously.

Falling to the floor I lunged for the telephone, in an attempt to call the police. Before I could dial the "O" for the operator, his fist reached my stomach, and caused me excruciating pain, loss of breath, and nausea. With the bit of strength that I could muster, I crashed the receiver into his head and face. He stumbled and fell momentarily, allowing me enough time to complete the call for police assistance. "Operator", I screamed, "my husband is trying to kill me," please send the police to 2859 K Street, 2859 K Street!" Throwing the phone down to the floor, I ran towards the back door, and proceeded down the street. I looked back as I approached the corner, and saw Larry on my trail. I turned the corner, and about half-way down the block I saw flashing lights and heard the police sirens.

Exhausted I stopped running as I heard the police on the loudspeaker requesting me to stop. The police had Larry sitting in the back seat handcuffed. He was yelling out profanities from the police car.

"B--- I'll get you and you will be sorry you ever met me! You are a ugly, black, B----, and I hate you! These people cannot keep me in jail!"

The police asked me what happened? A ludicrous quesion, I thought. It took very few observational skills to see that my eyes were swollen shut and bloody from Larry's beating. They had found him chasing me down the street, threatening my life. The police told me that they were taking Larry to prison, and would hold him for a cooling off period of twenty four hours. By this time, all of our neighbors were either peeping from their windows or standing on the street looking at us. I was so ashamed, I hung my head and started walking to our house.

In the midst of the confusion, I had forgotten that I left our son sound asleep at the house. Running hastily to the house that was sitting with both doors wide open, I rushed to his bedroom, and to my surprise he was not in his crib. As I went to the telephone to call the police again, my next door neighbor, Sue Lin, knocked on the door. I opened the door to find that she had my son in her arms. Hurriedly, I reached for my son, and told Sue Lin, thank you. I was so ashamed, I didn't desire to talk or explain anything to anyone.

I telephoned my parents in New Orleans to inform them of what had happened, and to request that they would wire me sufficient funds to come home. Mother and Daddy understood what I was going through, and promised to send a money telegram on the next day.

As I looked in the bathroom mirror, my features were so distorted. My eyes were almost swollen shut, and my face deformed, due to constantly being hit in the face. After calming and feeding our son, I put him in bed, I started packing our clothing for our trip back to New Orleans. As I packed, my thoughts were full of anger, hurt, and bitterness. I desired to take out revenge, and to repay Larry for what he had done to me. I desired to hurt him even more than I was hurt. My thoughts were absorbed with scenes of me going to his job on base, and shoot him until every bullet in our pistol was discharged, and Larry was dead.

He had consistently battered me and I felt so helpless and defeated. I just wanted out of the entire situation, I'd had enough. With thoughts of revenge, murder, and escape crowding my mind, exhausted, I fell asleep.

I Cried For Help
And No One Helped

Suddenly I sat up in bed, awakened by the sound of breaking glass! Before I could get out of my room to investigate, Larry appeared in the bedroom doorway. He was screaming to the top of his voice, "B----, you thought the police would hold me, didn't you?" He grabbed me by my hair and flung me to the floor. I could hear our son crying, he had been awakened by Larry's yelling.

He began to kick me in my stomach and in the back. As I attempted to cover an injured portion of my body, he'd find an opening and either kick me with his feet or punch me with his fists. I screamed in pain, calling out for help! But there was no one to respond to my outcry. My pain was so intense, that at some point I just wanted it to be over. Larry continued his brutal physical attack on me in retaliation for my calling the police on him.

I do not recall how long this beating took place. In my mind the punching and kicking would never cease. I screamed and cried, "please stop, please stop, I am sorry, I'll do whatever you tell me, I'll never call the police again, I'm sorry, please, please!" His response, to my pitiful pleading was, "You are sorry, I should never have married you, my Mother warned me about black a-- women, Mother said that this marriage would never work". Finally he stopped punching, slapping, and kicking me.

Lying on the floor bleeding and battered, my attention shifted to our screaming son in the other bedroom. I attempted to get up off the floor, and get our son, to comfort him. Agonizingly, I attempted to lift myself from the floor. Larry placed his foot on my head preventing me from moving. Larry said, "You are a dirty b----, and I don't want your filthy hands on my son." He went to the baby's room, and brought him back to our bedroom. Instinctively, our son reached for me to console him. Larry said, "Don't touch this baby m----- f----- you are a no good w----." Our son continued crying and reaching for me.

Larry became so irritated that he screamed, "Get the hell out of my sight!"

Broken, weeping, in pain, humiliated, I managed to drag my battered body from our bedroom to the bathroom. There I locked the door, pulled myself up to sit on the commode, where I could wash my face. Horrified at what peered back at me in the mirror, I dropped to the floor crying.

There I made a mental affirmation, that when I got out of this situation, I would <u>never</u> allow any man to do this to me again. There I affirmed that I would leave Larry, and it didn't matter how long it would take me. I resolved that I would <u>never</u> reconcile with him again. I swore to get even with Larry for these merciless, barbarous attacks.

Til Death Do Us Part,
I Think Not

I decided this was not the kind of treatment that I desired to receive until death do us part. Larry never offered to take me to the hospital where I could get medical attention for my injuries, blackened eyes, busted lips, headaches, pains in the chest, stomach and back, neither would he permit me to go to the medical dispensary. Larry feared that he would be prosecuted for assault and battery, and possibly dishonorably discharged from the US Navy.

Larry went to work each day from 7:00AM to 4:30PM. Fear and intimidation kept me locked down physically, however mentally, I continued to plan and strategize my inevitable departure. The money that I had requested from Mother and Daddy came in the mail several days after this incident. Opportunity to implement my plans came about four months later. Larry had weekend duty aboard the ship. This meant Larry had to work from 7:00 AM, on Friday, until the following Monday at 4:30PM. This time frame allotted me over 72 hours to hold a garage sale of our personal home furnishings, pack our clothing, and purchase train tickets for myself and my son to escape this madness.

The garage sale was successful. Most non-commissioned officers and their families had to live off meager pay, and were glad for the opportunity to purchase anything for several dollars or less. I sold all the living and bedroom furniture, the linen closet contents, pots, pans, dishes, flatware, the stove and refrigerator.

During the sixties, the $1000 dollars I made from the sale of all our household items was a lot of money. Due to Larry's insecurities, he called on the telephone every hour when he was absent from home. Whenever he called, the house was full of chattering women bartering for a bargain price, I would make sure that they were quieted before I answered the phone. Calmly, I would answer the telephone, and communicate with Larry in a calm, civil, voice. Afterward, the ladies and I would return to business as usual.

Sue Lin, my Philippine neighbor next door, assisted me by packing our clothing, taking our luggage to the train station, purchased our train ticket, and checking our luggage on the Sunset Limited train, service from San Diego, California to New Orleans, Louisiana.

Sue Lin was a very beautiful, olive complexion Asian lady with dark almond shaped eyes and a beautiful personality. Sue Lin, was married to a Caucasian, man named Steve, whom she met on a bus in Manila. Steve was enlisted as a US Marine. Inevitably they started courting and became married. Sue told me that she remembered the day and night of the attacks that Larry subjected me to. She recalled that early morning sound of breaking glass that awakened her and Steve. Sue Lin confided in me that she had heard my cries for help, and began to have flashbacks of her Mother crying for help under the physical attacks of her Dad. She said the same feelings of helplessness, anger, and fear crowded her mind when she heard Larry's verbal, vulgar, abuse to me. Sue apologized to me for not coming to my assistance, and not calling the police for help, but when she started to call for help, her husband told her that she should not become involved. For this she profusely apologized, and did more than compensate to me for her perceived guilt. Due to her consistent help during the entire weekend, I was able to leave Larry in a timely manner, without his suspecting my plans. After the garage sale was complete, everything was sold except Larry's clothing and our car.

On the Monday that he was to return home from weekend duty at 4:30 PM, I boarded the Sunset Limited at 10:30 AM bound for New Orleans, Louisiana. I learned from Sue Lin in a letter that the evening Larry returned home, he asked throughout the neighborhood where I had gone and where had I put his furniture. Sue Lin sort of felt sorry for Larry, because not one of the neighbors gave him any information. Hurriedly, I read over the part about her sympathy for Larry, and thanked God that I had escaped without loss of limb or life.

Even though I never physically reconciled with Larry, whenever he was granted furlough, he would travel to New Orleans to see me. My parents were never aware that Larry was in town, until it became obvious that I was pregnant. My parents were very displeased that I had agreed to see Larry in light of all the physical abuse. But I guess they felt helpless to prohibit me. In order to see Larry without having to explain to my parent, I moved into my own rented house.

Unfortunately these caustic experiences did not end with my separation from Larry. After several years of attempting reconciliation and three children later, I finally resolved that I would not permit Larry to come to visit me in New Orleans anymore.

Consequently, when I was separated physically from the abuser, the caustic experiences lingered in other aspects of my life.

On The Job

"There is a signal 64-G that cars 604, 602, and 610 are currently responding to. Did anyone make the coffee? The switchboard relief has not arrived and the 7 AM to 3 PM folks want some relief. Joe, will you relieve these ladies? Who is the Watch Commander for the 3 PM to 11 PM? Channel C will be manned by Eunique. Sergeant Howard, who is assigned to Channels A and B? Are the natives restless tonight in the Fifth and Sixth Districts? Sergeant Howard, the Fire Department is on the line to discuss the fire reported on the Police Communications line." These sounds accompanied the change of shifts at the New Orleans Police Department. On a typical weekday night, I worked the 3-11 shift.

Yoacum, a white policeman who worked in the Communications Center, came to my usual station to see if Mona and I had relieved the 7 AM to 3 PM PBX (private band exchange) switchboard. Mona was a white lady in her early sixties. She was the sweetest, kindest, most generous white person that I have ever met. She had a beautiful spirit. She had an unusual laugh when she laughed real hard her bladder relaxed and she 'd get her clothing wet. There was a standing joke in the office as to whether Mona had brought a change of clothing. Yoacum, was a short, pot bellied, blond haired, white man who told all the Black women working in the Communications Center that he wished to be addressed as Mr. or Officer Yoacum. That was fine with me as long as the titles used when addressing me, were Mrs. or Officer.

I was hired by the New Orleans Police Department in February of 1967. Even before I had any assignments, there were three strikes against me. I was (1) a female, (2) a Black female, (3) an outspoken Black female.

At the height of the Civil Rights protests, I found myself employed by an organization whose purpose was to uphold the law, that in fact was perpetuating the antagonistic, unjust, biased, treatment of African Americans. During these times many of our white male officers and their wives were threatned by the presence of women sharing the same car as their husbands for an eight hour tour of duty, five days a week. The wives main complaint was their concerns about the sanctity and preservation of their marriages. The men were concerned that a female could not sufficiently protect them as a partner, as it was common knowledge that we were "the weaker sex." Both of the statements were ludicrous. Many of the married cops were already involved in extra-marital affairs.

At the height of the Civil Rights demonstrations, four Black women were hired to receive police complaint calls from citizens requesting police assistance. I was one and the other three were, Eunique, Gail, and Rayann. Eunique was a very quiet unassuming "Creole" woman in her late thirties. Creoles in New Orleans are of black and white parentage. Eunique could have easily passed for a Caucasian woman. She once confided in me that she had a brother who lived in California that was passing for white.

Eunique never responded to the nasty innuendoes or racial bashing that took place in the Communications Center. Gail, was in her early forties, a jovial woman who had once considered becoming a nun in the Catholic church. Gail was as hurt by the racial bashing as I was, but opted not to react. Rayann, was just out of high school, and appeared to be very diligent in her position and sought to advance in her police career. I was the only one in the Communications department that put up a defense against the ugly, nasty, obscene, crude, disgusting, racial insults that were hurled against Black people.

As the first Black females to be hired in the New Orleans Police Department-Communications Division, we were the recipient of many racial jokes, innuendoes, and outright disgusting racial comments. My unique ability to answer these agitations in the most articulate, vocal, coarse, manner did not enhance my congeniality status. One standing joke for someone to yell, "Hey you!' I would look, although my Mother gave me a name other than you. Then I would be pointed at "Yes you!" "Is it true that nig---- don't eat anything but red beans and chicken, and that is why they smell like sh--?" My crude response was, "Ask your Mother, she would know!"

The forbidden word n----- was used blatantly and often. Other Black communications police staff did not respond to these insults. They merely became absorbed in their assigned duties and ignored the comments. Even the commanding officers of the communications center did not order the harassment and racial bashing to end. We were constantly bombarded with name-calling such as "jungle bunny, black sambo, big lips, stupid nig----, a-- holes, and mo---- f-----s. My co-workers hung their heads in humiliation, but I retaliated with, "stupid crackers, honky mother f------, poor white trash, silly son of a b----, ignorant a--ho--s," and a variety of other choice nasty words.

There is an old saying, "Sticks and stones may break my bones, but words will never hurt me." That is one of the most inaccurate statements that has ever been made. Words do in fact hurt, an untamed hurting tongue can do more long term damage than a bullet or a knife.

During the late 60s the Police Department decided that too many police personnel were not being assigned to street, detective, or police work. They wanted to introduce non-police personnel to do the office work that policemen and women were now doing. The local paper advertised for the position of Police Communications Clerk. I had just had our fourth child, and was recuperating from the pressures of having a dysfunctional marriage. I was trying to bring closure to a relationship that was physically, verbally, and mentally abusive, and my body was trying to heal.

The written test was administered through the Civil Service Commission at City Hall in New Orleans. Three weeks went by and no word from the Commission, so I assumed that I was not one of the successful candidates. Instead of receiving a written notice in the mail to the effect that I had either passed or failed the test, I received a telephone call from the New Orleans Police Department that requested me to come to their Personnel office for processing as a new hire for the position of Communications Clerk. I was elated.

Larry made several attempts to reconcile our marriage. By then I realized all hope for us remaining married was futile. We were now the parents of two boys and two girls. I remained in New Orleans, and opted not to live with or have sexual relations with Larry after our fourth child was born. My new born daughter was only one month and two days old when I began work at the police department.

The form of training we received was to be handed a card, about the size of a post card with police codes and classifications on both sides. We were instructed to commit these codes and classifications to memory. The New Orleans Police Department Communications Center is the heartbeat of the police department. In this sphere of duty, police assistance was dispatched to citizens calling into the communications center. This center existed prior to 911 computerized dispatch centers.

If there was an armed robbery taking place, it was the duty of the person that manned the Automatic Call Distributor (ACD) position to record as much detail as could be obtained from the person calling in, such as a description of the perpetrators, the location of the offense (address), how many persons were involved, what type of weapon did they observe, what kind/color of clothing is worn by the robbers, is anyone injured, are the robbers still in the place being robbed? Were the perpetrators black or white? Did you observe an automobile? If so, what color, did you record or memorize a license number?

This manner of questions was very difficult to obtain from the calling party. The person calling the police was usually in an agitated frame of mind and normally wanted to scream out the location of the offense, and became more agitated when questioned. However, the answers to these questions were important, in order to determine the coding and classification of the call.

Coding was the system used to determine what degree of crisis the call entailed. Classification was the part of the Criminal/Civil law that was allegedly being violated. If the assailants were holding up a place of business with a gun, then this call would be classified as a 64-G, code 2. 64-G indicated to the police officers that an armed robbery with a gun was the type of crime. Code 2 meant for them to get to the destination dispatched on the radio using flashing blue lights, and as speedily as possible considering their own safety and the safety of other motorists.

One incident I specifically remember was at the height of the Civil Rights Protests. The New Orleans Police Department's Communications Center was located in the Criminal Courts building at Tulane and Broad streets. It was reported on television, radio, the Civil Rights activist, H. R.

Brown was planning a visit to the New Orleans area. H. R. Brown was the President of the Student Non-Violent Coordinating Committee in the late sixties. He was made an honorary member of the Black Panther Party in 1967. The Black Panther Party was a group of young, angry Black men and women who thought they could change the world, and in the course of ten years, they did. They were articulate, sincere, educated, revolutionaries that presented a new model of Black political, and social activism.

We were told by the Chief of Police that we were to work twelve hour tours of duty until further instructed. I was very excited about H.R. Brown coming to New Orleans. My thoughts were, finally someone would put these white folks in

79

their place. Finally, we as Black people would experience some justice. I had made up my mind that I would participate in some of the Civil Rights marches, sit-ins, and protests. That thought was soon aborted, when the Chief of Police told us that we were prohibited from participation in any of the demonstrations. The more I thought about this mandate the more I realized that the twelve hour tour of duty would seriously hinder any participation in these demonstrations.

However, the reactions of my white co-workers were fear, agitation, distress, and tension. I kept a smile on my face, and was even pleasant to my agitators. I finally realized they were fearful when I heard the jokes about me protecting them and informing the Party that they were "all right blue eyed devils". For a fleeting moment I felt sorry and even pitied them. On the other hand, some of my white co-workers were arrogantly bragging, "If those ni----s get in here, I'm shooting to kill all of their as---!" At that moment I marveled that one Black man could cause so much intimidation, induce so much fear, and drive an entire city to arm themselves for war.

The windows at the Criminal Court building and the New Orleans Police Department Communications Center were boarded with plywood. Armed police personnel were stationed at all possible entrances to the building, and barbed wire was strategically placed at the entrance of the underground garage.

Police cars were specially equipped with rifles, policemen were fitted with bullet proof jackets. In reality we were on civil alert. Civil Defense vehicles, and US Army jeeps held army personnel armed with rifles and explosive devices. Armored tanks rolling through the streets of New Orleans were visible, it seemed, at every intersection in the Black and White neighborhoods.

The cold winter humid air was charged with anxiety. With assured anticipation I sat each twelve hour shift awaiting the arrival of the notorious H. R. Brown. I pondered in my mind wouldn't it be great if New Orleans experienced some of the great demonstrations that had occurred in Alabama and Mississippi? Civil rights were certainly an issue in our city, as it was in the entire United States. However, New Orleans was so built that if there was a riot, God forbid, both Black and White neighborhoods would be equally affected. For instance, on one street there were very majestic plantations where the wealthy White families resided, and on the next block over, sometimes with backyards joining, were the not so noble Black residences.

During Reconstruction, these houses were conveniently built so that the white slave masters could keep watch over their slave possessions. Now, however, in light of the anticipated riots this building strategy was not favorable. It was a common saying that New Orleans would never have a race riot, because people couldn't tell if in fact the house they were burning belonged to their relatives.

Anxiously, I awaited the day when H. R. Brown and his band of soldiers would come to New Orleans. Each day after my twelve hour shift, when the Black Panther Party had not entered nor come near the city, I went home disappointed. New Orleans Police, US Army, Civil Defense employees, The Auxiliary New Orleans Police, Louisiana State Police, Orleans & Jefferson Parish Sheriff Departments were kept on standby.

As the days passed, tensions mounted within the Communication Center, nerves were frayed, co-workers were intolerant and irritable to each other. I sat back and observed fear raging through my white fellow colleagues. I was informed enough about riots to know that if the Black Panther Party did come to New Orleans, there was a possibility that I could be seriously injured or die. I soon dismissed the thought and replaced it with a more pleasant hope, that we as a people would finally be treated as human beings and not as animals.

The next morning, as I returned home from work, I gave the possibility of my being injured of killed more thought. I decided I'd call Mother and request her prayers, as well as give

81

her instructions regarding the well-being of my children. As I drove across the Mississippi River Bridge, for a rare moment, I reflected on what would happen to my children in the event of my dying. Would they be reared by Larry? Larry's parents? Mother and Daddy? Then I thought, Larry? No, he had been arrested for being (AWOL) absent without leave.

Larry became angry with me when I pursued an allotment check from the military for child support. So I guess he figured the only way to get out of paying, and to requite me for refusing to reconcile, was to get out of the military. Larry's parents? That certainly would not be my wish. Larry and his parents maintained an indifferent relationship the entire time we were married. We initiated a trip to Mississippi to allow them to see their first grandchild in the early sixties, but they never wrote, telephoned, or visited. So my obvious answer was they were not an option.

My sister Mae, was living in Washington, DC. She and her husband were raising three sons of their own. My other sister had relocated to Detroit, Michigan with her husband, and they were expecting twins-their fourth and fifth child, so they were not good candidates. As my alternatives narrowed I came to my parents. Mother still did domestic work and Daddy was contemplating retirement. Not thinking of their ages, their plans, or their lives, I concluded they were the only conceivable people available to take over the rearing of my children if I died.

Hurriedly, I raced the 1965 Ford station wagon across the Mississippi River Bridge to telephone Mother with what thoughts and decisions I'd made. She answered the phone in her normal sweet manner "Hello." I said, "Hi, Mother, how are you today?" She must have heard the anxiety in my voice, and she inquired, "Is everything all right?" "Yes, I've been thinking about what would happen to me if I was to be killed in the line of duty." She said, "What provoked those thoughts?" I explained to her what was happening at my job, and how driving home from work I thought about the future of my children in the event of my death. She replied, "Dear, it is good that you are thinking ahead, but I believe that you will live a long life and that the good Lord will permit you to raise your children....."

"Mother," I interrupted, "No one knows what the next day will bring!" Having gotten her attention, I was able to tell her about the pension plan and insurance the kids would be eligible to receive, and that she and Daddy would not be financially strapped or have to use their own personal funds to take care of the children. Her response was, "Pansy, everything will be just fine. That man Mr. Brown, probably will not set foot in New Orleans." Little did I know that, as usual, Mother was absolutely right. Neither H. R. Brown, nor any other members of the Black Panther Party, came to New Orleans.

Obviously, someone on the inside tipped him off, or may-be the Black Panthers never intended to come to New Orleans, but allowed that tidbit of information to get out so that the authorities might be thrown off their trail. Unfortunately, circum-stances on the job did not improve. The racial jokes, name-calling, narrow-mindedness, and pitiless, pointless, aggravation persisted. The silence of my Black co-workers continued, and I continued to produce a stream of indecent, insensitive, insult-ing responses. After three years tenure on the job, there was never a moment that I was allowed to forget that I was a Black woman on a White police force.

One evening, while working in the Communications Center on the Complaint Desk, I received a call from a woman who complained that there was a fight in the 500 block of Fern Street. I asked the caller whether there were any weapons involved in the fight? She responded, "No," I asked who was fighting, she responded, "Children, and they are in the middle of the street, you better send the police right away!" I asked, "Are they white kids, black kids, what color clothing are they wearing?" By this time she had become quite aggravated with me, and replied, "What damn difference does it make? Just send the damned police!" With this last statement she unceremoniously hung up the telephone.

Hanging up the telephone was not unusual behavior for a citizen requesting police assistance. It was their mind set, why are you asking all these foolish questions? Just send the police!!! I wrote the complaint up as a 103-f, code 1. A 103 was the signal for disturbing the peace, the f indicated that the disturbance was a fight, and code 1 was the manner in which the police were to respond to the complaint. Code 1 was the normal manner, no flashing blue lights, no speeding, just a normal, non-emergency response.

Two weeks later, as I walked in the Communications Center to take my normally assigned position, I was stopped by Sgt. Howard. He said, "Pansy, I need to talk with you." My response was, "OK, Sarge let me put my things down." Sgt. Howard was a mild-mannered White policeman, who supervised the 3 PM to 11 PM shift. He was not at all like the rest of the White policemen. Whenever the racial bashing would became too hot, he would intervene, saying, "That is enough!" However he was affected by the assumption that Blacks were inferior. He gained this from inaccurate teaching taught in his church, that Black people were a result of a curse that God had placed on them. I disagreed with this even though I did not know how to prove him wrong from the Word of God.

As I approached Sgt. Howard, he was seated reading the newspaper. Peering over his horn rimmed glasses, he asked, "Have you read today's paper?" "No, is there something I should see?" He said, "Sit down. I have something I must discuss with you." We were in a huge room that housed the complaint desk, the four police radio channels, and the Command post where we sat—not a private office, but a desk in the Communications Division. He opened his desk drawer and pulled out some papers, and began to tell me about the complaint on Fern Street, and the newspaper article he was reading.

Sgt. Howard stated that I had coded and classified the call incorrectly. The woman who initiated the call to the police became very upset, when the police did not respond in what she considered a timely manner. So she complained to the local newspaper. The room grew strangely quiet as he continued. The local newspaper picked up the story, called the Chief of Police and complained. Sgt. Howard continued, "I've been instructed by the Chief of Police and the Internal Affairs Bureau to suspend you until a full investigation is completed."

When the White policemen on our shift heard this, they literally cheered and hooted, "We are finally rid of the ni---- bi---!!!" Sgt. Howard told me to pick up my personal things, turn in my badge identification, and keys. He further instructed me that I would be escorted off the premises per orders from the Chief of Police.

Job Suspension With
Five Mouths To Feed

I was shocked, humiliated, and at a complete loss for words. Shocked, because I had no forewarning, no progressive discipline, just leave! Humiliated, because my tormentors were rejoicing over my hurt and pain, my inability to respond to the accusations, my complete shame and perplexity. Here I was stripped of my job, my self-esteem in front of my foes.

Hurriedly, head hanging, I left the articles that my Commanding Officer had requested. I wanted the floor to open and swallow me up, as I was escorted out of the New Orleans Police Department's premises. I cried as I got into my car to drive home, why was it I found no words to respond to the accusations? Me? The articulate one? Humbled to a motionless, speechless, lifeless human being!!

During my nine months of suspension, I did muster up enough self-respect to file for a hearing with the Civil Service Commission. While on suspension, naturally my concerns were, how was I to pay the mortgage, buy food, purchase clothing for my children, pay utility bills, make furniture payments, and maintain our quality of living? The only alternative that I had was to apply for welfare assistance.

So while I searched the want ads for alternative employment, we received a monthly stipend from the welfare—not enough money to pay for the mortgage. Without assistance from my parents, and food stamps, I would have defaulted on my mortgage. As it was, our gas, water, and electricity, were periodically disconnected due to non-payment.

My Day In Court

Finally my day in court came. I paid particular attention to my dress, as I did not want to appear for the hearing looking like Lil Orphan Annie. I wore a white dress with black polka dots, with a black collar and cuffs, and black shoes and purse. I was not represented by an attorney. However, all the attorneys representing the New Orleans Police Department, the Chief of Police, Sgt. Howard, several white policemen, the press, the lady who initiated the telephone call and her neighbors, the staff of the Internal Affairs of the New Orleans Police, and a female white co-worker were all present and accounted for to give testimony against me.

To say that I was intimidated was an understatement. More like frightened half out of my wits would have better described my state of mind that day. I remained seated as they filed one by one into the New Orleans City Council Chambers where the hearing would be held.

The Civil Service Commission was a board of citizens utilized to arbitrate complaints against the Police. It consisted of seven members, four men and three women, all White. One by one they all testified to the infamous event that had occurred on Fern Street. It appeared as the other parts of the story unfolded, that a two- man police car had responded to the call. Further testimony by the officers reported that there was a fight going on in the street between Whites and Blacks. I was accused of being militant, and possibly involved in some civil rights organization. Because I was not represented by an attorney, there was no objection to this type of accusation. My character, as reported by my co-workers was questionable, but the quality of my work during my tenure with the Police Department was reported to be impeccable.

There was this one little chubby White man sitting on the Commission, who took notes feverishly, and cross-examined each of the witnesses presented by the Police Department. Finally the time came for the tapes from the Complaint Desk to be heard by the Commission. The tapes revealed that I was not the first police personnel to answer a complaint call for the same address, but I was the only personnel that had been suspended.

A White clerk had taken a call before me. The Clerk, Sandy, testified she had coded and classified the complaint in the same manner as I had. Now it was time for the Chief of Police to testify. He was asked about the training that was administered to the Police and civilian personnel. His response was, "They are trained, but the civilian personnel could never be as informed as the Police personnel." The little chubby White commission member took issue with his statement, and challenged the Chief of Police. He asked him, "What are you saying, is the Chief of Police providing a separate type of training for Police personnel and civilian clerks?"

The Chief became so angry at that question that he became visibly shaken, and his countenance turned red. Before the Chief could answer, this little chubby white man stamped his gavel, and said, "A blind man could see that this is a witch hunt and I am not buying into it! This woman is to be re-instated to her prior position with full retroactive pay, with accrued annual and sick leave!" The entire Civil Service Commission agreed, and the hearing was adjourned.

I was in total shock. Even though I felt as though I had done nothing to deserve suspension. I had persuaded myself that my co-workers would fabricate trumped-up charges and the Civil Service Commission would uphold the charges and inevitably I would be permanently terminated.

After the hearing was adjourned, I was attempting to leave the building, when the Communications Clerk called out to me. "Congratulations, Pansy, when will you be returning to work?" In all of the excitement, I had forgotten to ask Sgt. Howard what date I was to report for duty. Hurriedly, I walked towards the elevator to see if I could locate him. Obviously, he had slipped through the crowds and was gone.

However, the news media was very present, surrounding the Chief of Police questioning him about the disposition of the hearing. I heard him saying that the policewoman was vindicated and reinstated to duty. With that statement he brushed off any further questions, and got in the elevator that I had boarded.

I looked at him and said. "Thank you." He said, "For what? I didn't do anything." I told the Chief that I was attempting to catch up with Sgt. Howard, but missed him. I needed to know when I was to report to work? Strangely, he responded, "If it had been left to me, you would have no work to go to forever." Unwilling to believe what I heard I replied, "What on earth for?" He looked me squarely in the face and said, " I believe you are militant and a disgrace to the uniform, and the department that you work in, and not fit to be a police officer." My scathing response was,

"Why didn't you say that while the press was interviewing you?" I'm a disgrace? No, you are the disgrace!" With that comment the elevator was at the main floor.

As I disembarked, he yelled, "Come to work on Monday we will be waiting for you!" I thought, as I turned around to see a sneering grin on his face, what in the hell is that supposed to mean?

Monday I returned to work and was reinstated without incident. Later on in the day, I was requested to report to the payroll department to verify my accrued sick and annual leave days. On my way back downstairs to the Communications department, I encountered some fellow Black policemen who had heard of my victory, and they gave me congratulatory hugs, and well wishes.

Approximately two weeks later, I received my retroactive pay for the nine months that I was suspended from active duty in addition to my regular pay, totaling over fifteen thousand dollars.

On the weekend that followed, I purchased a brand-new Ford Convertible Torino. The following Monday at work, as I parked my brand new automobile, I observed some of my co-workers enviously looking at me and my new car. I realized that my career was over with the New Orleans Police Department. I knew that the harassment would continue, and because I'd won my appeal, there would be a concerted effort by my co-workers as well as the Chief of Police to terminate me. I returned to work this last day to submit my letter of resignation, and to show my co-workers the car that they had allowed me to purchase, paid in full.

In The Family

Having five children was a full-time job for me, in addition to my employment, I was also attempting to go to school. Life, in my estimation, had been good to me. However, it was increasingly more difficult for me to lease an apartment or house for me and my family. I think prospective landlords considered that families with over two children were a sure route to a lot of extra repairs on their properties.

This led me into seeking to buy my own house. A four-bedroom two-bath house became available, across the street from my parents' home. It was ideal for me and the kids, we could remain close to my aging parents, and still live in a nice big house.

Mother was still working, but Daddy had retired and was going to need surgery. After surgery, he recovered and started cooking for a group of men who went on hunting/fishing excursions quarterly. Daddy and Mother were pleased with this arrangement, as it afforded him an opportunity to earn additional money within the guidelines of Social Security, and it was not as laborious as a forty-hour a week job. The fishing/hunting expeditions lasted for three weeks, every three months.

Daddy's face reflected the immense satisfaction he received after returning from these trips. His face absolutely lit up, as he shared stories of catches and kills. He always brought home an ample amount of fish and deer meat from his travels. Shortly after returning from a hunting trip in North Louisiana, Daddy became ill. He remarked to me, "I am just tired, as soon as I get some rest, I'll be fine."

Finally came the closing date for my house. I was a home owner, and my family and I moved out of my parents home into our own home. I was excited, at the age of twenty-five years old, I had purchased our first home. I worked feverishly on my days off in order to get the place painted, and purchase

91

the furniture necessary to complete the look that I desired. The entire home was approximately twenty-five hundred square feet, which included living/dining room, four bedrooms, two bathrooms, kitchen, den, and utility room. As the kids and I dragged box after box across the street, and unpacked them the new furniture was being delivered.

In less than two weeks the inside of our home had been painted, furniture purchased, and our move was completed. Mother was a great help in assisting me to coordinate every aspect of our move. Daddy had never seen the inside of the house; he was still resting and sleeping a lot. In the same month that I moved into our new home, three weeks to the day, Daddy died.

Grief could not accurately describe my loss. I was devastated. For five months, I could not recall how I existed. My loss was so severe to me, I did not take the time to realize my Mother's sorrow. How I passed mid-term exams, worked an eight hour a day job, and managed to take care of my children during that period was an act of HIS grace. Words cannot adequately express my loss of my Daddy, friend, confidante, and chief supporter. Whenever it was necessary for me to work until 11:00 PM Daddy would get on the bus and retrieve my children from the baby-sitter. Mother stayed at the house to meet my older ones from school. Daddy had convinced Mother to buy me a car. The commute was too strenuous for me to get from work to school and home on the bus.

Daddy hadn't lived long enough to drive the automobile that he had purchased for me. After his surgery, he had a tumor that was lodged in his back between his ribs. The doctors told us that the surgery was successful, and that Daddy would be fine. No one suspected that Daddy would die.

I recall, after I moved across the street from my parents, Daddy began telling me some family recipes and secret ingredients that made him a very sought-after cook, but not for a moment did I realize that these words would be his final input into my life. Perhaps, if I had been prepared, I would not have taken his death so hard. Loss of weight, appetite, depression, memory lapses, were all symptomatic of the grief that I bore for the loss of my Daddy. Meanwhile Mother was comforting my sisters and myself that Daddy would not have wanted us to brood as we were doing, but to go on with our lives.

One day, as I walked down the street on my way home from the neighborhood grocery, I looked up and saw this lady walking ahead of me. She was heading towards the corner. To my surprise, as she turned the corner, I realized that this lady, was my Mother.

I hadn't recognized her because the woman I walked behind was short and of a medium frame. My Mother was short, but she was stout. My Mother wore a size 24 1/2 dress, this woman appeared to be a size 14-16. I yelled, "Mother"? She turned around and said, "Yes?" It was at this moment that I realized that my Mother's grief was even more severe than mine. She had lost her husband, lover, provider, and friend of over forty three years. It was that experience that caused me to quit being so concerned about my loss, and to focus on the only parent that I had left in this world, my Mother.

As time progressed, the grief slowly healed, and I began to move back into my customary way of life. On this particular morning, I was awakened by the jangling noise of the doorbell. I sat up perplexed, it was only 5:00 AM. Staggering to the door, I yelled, "Who is it?" The response came back, "It's Glenda!" "Glenda, Glenda who?" "Glenda Eugene, your classmate in high school." "Glenda girl, what are you doing here this time of morning?" I asked, opening the door. "Come in, is everything all right?" She said, "Pansy, I am sorry to wake you at this hour of the morning. To answer your question, everything is well with me and my family. However, I've been up all night. The couple down the street had a fight and it kept the entire block up all night, until somebody got tired and called the police! The man beat his wife, chased her out of their house and she had no clothing on!"

"The woman has just moved into our neighborhood and doesn't know any of her neighbors yet. He chased her across several lawns, and she was screaming for help with her little girl running behind her. It was sad, and every door she went to no one opened the door for her, or would let her in.

I am standing in my window watching the whole thing. Her husband caught her by the hair and began to beat her, she was screaming, someone please help me, call the police. Her husband began calling her all types of filthy names, he threw her to the ground and she must have kicked him in his groin, because momentarily he dropped to his knees bent over.

This gave her enough time to cross the street and as she crossed the lawn, I heard knocks and cries of desperation, and I opened the door for her. Her little daughter was several feet behind her, so I called out to her to come saying, your Mommy is here! Hurriedly, I locked the doors and called the police! Within seconds, the husband was at my door, yelling and screaming for his wife to come out or he would break the door down and get her. By this time, girl I was shaking in my boots! When he threatened to kick my door in, I told him, I have called the police and told them who you are, what you are wearing, and given them your address, so get away from my door and off my property!

Just then I could see the flashing blue lights as the police approached my house. Mr. bad man, the bully, ran across the street back to his own house. The police came to my house, took a report of the incident, and advised Sarah and I that this was a civil matter and the police had no jurisdiction in a civil matter. When they were reminded that the bruises and cuts that Sarah received from her husband, were a criminal matter namely, battery, the police consented to talking with her husband."

I was awake now, but not fully aware of what this had to do with me. I asked Glenda, "So how did I get involved in all this?" I poured us both a cup of coffee.

She said, "I came to ask you would you be willing to let her stay at your house until she can get herself together?"

"What's wrong with her staying at your house?"

"Well the husband knows where she is, and she doesn't put it beneath him to come back to my house and harass her, or to break into my house."

"So, girlfriend, what I hear you saying is that this joker will break into your house. Well, what in hell is going to stop him from attempting to break into my house?"

She answered, "Well for one thing he doesn't know where she is, and the other thing is that you have worked for the Police Department, and I figured you could ask them to keep an eye on your place."

As I thought about her request, flashbacks of Larry fighting me flashed in my mind, my feelings of hopelessness and helpless inundated my thoughts. Remembering how there was no one to run to, no one to help or comfort me, I heard my own voice saying, "Tell Sarah she and her daughter are welcome to stay with us as long as she needs to get herself together."

Glenda was elated, "I'll bring them over this afternoon when I get off work, is that all right with you?" She got up and went to the door thanking me giving me a big hug. "Sarah and Cindy will be a help to you and your family."

After Glenda left I got back in the bed and made an attempt to catch up with the sleep I'd been deprived of. Sleep evaded me. In its place were thoughts of this unknown woman Sarah. I wondered if we would get along together? Is she a lazy woman? Is her child unruly? Will her abusive husband be coming to visit her and their child? Did she steal? Was she an alcoholic? Realizing that my attempts to regain the lost sleep were futile, I got up and began fixing breakfast for my children.

I was in between jobs and had to apply for welfare and food stamps, until I found suitable employment. Breakfast consisted of a bowl of oatmeal, bananas, and milk. While seated at the table, I explained to my children that we were to have house guests. That Miss Sarah and her daughter were to come and live with us until they find an appropriate place to live. My youngest daughter, in childlike innocence asked, "Are they living outdoors now?" Laughing I said, "No, the place where they were staying is not safe for them, so they will be with us until they find a place."

My kids accepted this readily, because in their minds this was an opportunity to place their chores on someone else's shoulders, and there would be another child in the house to play with. Jasmine, my oldest daughter, said, "The little girl will sleep in my room with me." Juleah, the middle daughter said, "Thats good because you sleep too bad anyway, and I'll have a bed all to myself." Jambila, the two year old, said, "I'll sleep with Mommy!"

Finally we decided that everyone would keep their current sleeping arrangements, and we would give Miss Sarah and her daughter Cindy the family room. The remainder of the day was spent rearranging furniture so that Sarah and Cindy might be comfortable in their new lodgings.

My sons, Byron and Gerard, proved to be quite the handy young men, for boys of ten and twelve years of age. Their main concern was the possibility of their having to baby-sit another girl, if Miss Sarah was a working Mom like I was. Quickly, I told them to my knowledge that Miss Sarah was not employed, but if she was, I knew that they would not mind
being a big brother to a little girl who had no brothers or sisters
. Reluctantly the boys agreed to help Miss Sarah with Cindy.

All of my apprehensions and hesitancy about Sarah and her daughter disappeared after one look at this thin, frail, shadow of a woman standing at the door with Glenda. Sarah was a small short, woman with big pretty eyes. When you looked deep into those eyes, the hurt and pain was quite visible. Sarah was a humble, frightened woman and Cindy her daughter appeared equally as fearful. My heart melted with compassion for Sarah and Cindy. After Glenda left we began to get our guests settled in their new accommodations. My children took a liking to Cindy right away, she was a petite, mahogany-complexioned child with big beautiful eyes and the longest eyelashes I've ever seen. Cindy was overwhelmed by all this new attention from my kids and preferred staying close to her Mother.

Sarah and I sat and talked. Sarah explained that she had married Joe right after he graduated from college. Joe was a local guy, New Orleans was his home, but he attended college in Akron, Ohio. Joe opted to return to Louisiana after their marriage, he felt his chances of obtaining a teaching position were better than they were in Ohio. Sarah was like me, very reluctant to move to a strange city, but her love for her husband soon dismissed those fears. She said, "There was no evidence that Joe would turn out to be a batterer in the three years of courtship before our marriage. Neither were there any telltale signs that he grew up in that type of environment."

Sarah said that shortly after they moved to New Orleans and Joe landed a job with the Orleans Parish School Board the abuse began, and has continued throughout their entire relationship, even during her pregnancy with Cindy. While we prepared dinner for our families, I watched Sarah. She was a nervous wreck. Whenever I asked for anything, she would jump immediately to get it, not even knowing where the article or food was stored. Sarah's hands shook visibly. It was obvious to me that she needed plenty of rest, but she wanted to try to work off her hyper-behavior by helping in any way she could in the house. Before dinner was completed, Sarah had excused herself from the table and proceeded to wash the pots and pans. I mentioned to Sarah that my kid's normal chores were to clean the kitchen after meals. Sarah said, While I'm

here they will not have to do that." Shouts of joy sprang forth
from my kids! Hooray! "Now we can watch TV a little longer
before bedtime." My response was, "Now Byron, you and
Gerard can drill each other in your Mathematics, and the girls
can take turns in assisting with Jasmine's Science project,
while Juleah and I brush up on our sewing skills." They were
not happy campers about my decision about their extra time.

In the following weeks Sarah cleaned the house from top
to bottom including the kitchen cabinets, the linen closet, and
the utility room. My attempts to tell her that this was not
necessary were futile, she insisted that some form of chore was
beneficial to her mental stability. Sarah was excellent at
crocheting. She crocheted me a beautiful throw for my bed,
and Jambila a lovely sweater and matching hat. She was just as
efficient at crochet as she was with her housekeeping skills.
Sarah and I got along real well together.

One day, as we were cooking collard greens, corn bread
and a pot of smoked neck bones, Sarah shared with me that she
had accepted Jesus Christ as her personal Savior, but since she
had married Joe, she had become slack in attending church,
because her husband never wanted her to attend. She said in
her effort to not provoke him, she consented to not attending
church. She reflected, "Maybe that is where I went wrong."

She began to tell me about having been baptized in the
Holy Ghost and speaking in tongues. Sarah said her two sisters
in Akron, Ohio were very much involved in their church and
were licensed Evangelists. Well I was reared in the church,
however, when Sarah began to discuss speaking in tongues, the
baptism of the Holy Ghost, and interpretation of those tongues
as God speaking to the church through a human I was lost.

Suspiciously, I listened to Sarah, as I thought in my
mind, this girl is crazy! Never in my entire Christian life
had I ever heard of any such nonsense, either in the church,
nor preached from the pulpits. I considered myself to be a

Christian. I believed in Jesus Christ. What was this new nonsense?

Sarah was very adamant about my needing baptism in the Holy Ghost. I teased her that she must have gotten this new thing from Casper, the friendly ghost! I threw my head back and roared in laughter. Now, I was not an attendee of church every Sunday, but I sang in the choir, and donated money to the church whenever a collection was taken up. What on earth more could there be? Sure, I had a lifestyle that permitted infidelity, but just about everyone in the church was doing the same thing! It was common knowledge that many of the deacons had wives, but were involved in extra-marital affairs with some of the choir members and ushers. Sarah questioned me as to whether or not I really was a Christian. Sarah did not have a great deal of scriptural knowledge. I challenged her to show me proof in the Bible where she could come to a con-clusion that I really was not a Christian. I was really angry and offended that Sarah could come to such a decision, doubting my salvation.

My thoughts again went ballistic. No, I did not invite Jack the Ripper into my home to be a house guest, nor was she a thief. She was not lazy, nor did she steal, but instead, I invited some religious freak, who was questioning the integrity of my relationship with Jesus. I was absolutely outraged with Sarah! I resented her accusations, and let her know in so many words. I asked her, "Sarah if I am not saved who are you to make that judgment, and where were your saved people when you were running around naked in your neighborhood?" "Why didn't your tongue talking group come to you aid?" "The very nerve of you to stand in my face and tell me that I am not a believer in Jesus!" Sarah became very nervous and defensive. She realized that I was terribly upset with her religious, judgmental accusations. She blurted out, "I did not mean to get you angry, nor did I intend harm, I was just sharing my experience with the Lord." "Your experience with Him is one thing but to cast doubt on someone else or to not believe that God could have an interaction with a person outside of your religious circle is wrong," I retorted.

By this time I could feel my anger towards her increase-ing. Her eyes became watery with tears, Sarah's hands were shaking as she said, "I know some people, an Elder of the church and his wife, whom I've kept in contact with, Elder and Mrs. Smith. I am not very knowledgeable about the Bible, maybe they would consent to coming to your home to teach Bible classes, if that is all right with you?" "As long as they have wisdom enough to come in someone's home for the expressed purpose of teaching the Bible, and not to judge nor doubt their salvation."

Sarah apologized for offending me and retired to her room. Even though I had allowed Sarah to make me angry, in my heart I knew that my lifestyle was not consistent with what the Lord required. My rationale was that most every member of the church was involved in the same sin. I had forgiven Sarah and things at the house were back to normal. We did not discuss religion anymore, and the thoughts that I had doubting Sarah's sanity were carefully concealed.

Elder Smith was a slim, tall, gaunt looking man with eyes that were very deeply set in his head. His wife, Josephine, was a very heavy set woman, together they reminded me of the nursery rhyme.

"Jack Spratt could eat no fat, His wife could eat no lean, So both together they licked the platter clean."

Sister Curry, Josephine's Mother, was also a portly woman. The most obvious thing to me about this threesome was that the women did not wear any make up, and their skirts/dresses were ankle length. Sarah, in preparation for their coming to the house cooked a full meal that consisted of smothered pork chops with gravy, green peas and carrots, creamed potatoes, and a large salad of lettuce, tomatoes, cucumbers, and bell peppers. The house was filled with the fragrances of Sarah's food. Before they were even asked to have a seat and a proper introduction was made, the Elder's wife Josephine and Sister Curry were asking what was being cooked. Elder Smith appeared to be a bit more disciplined and mannerly, inviting them back into the living area reminding his wife that their fast would not end until 6:00 PM. After Sarah introduced me to Elder Smith, Josephine and Josephine's Mother, Sister Curry, we prayed and began Bible Study.

Elder Smith taught/preached out of the book of Romans. He had a different style of preaching, one that I had never encountered. He took his time to explain the who, what, when, where and how of the Bible. At the end of his teaching, Elder Smith prayed individually for me and my children. In his prayer for me, he asked that the Lord would save me and fill me with His precious Holy Ghost. When Elder Smith completed his prayers and Bible study was ended, I asked him if I could ask a question. He said, "Sure, ask on."

"In your prayer for me you asked the Lord to save me, as well as fill me with the Holy Ghost with the evidence of speaking in tongues?"

"Yes, I did."

"Why would you ask God to do something that he has done already? I am saved. I accepted the Lord Jesus Christ as a little girl. Now the Holy Ghost that you are referring to, I know nothing about, nor speaking in tongues. Is this something that is done in your church?"

Elder Smith answered "Yes, quite often."

It appeared as though he desired to say more, but paused to answer my question. He began by apologizing that he had assumed that I had not accepted Jesus Christ into my life. He continued, "You are absolutely correct, if you are saved there is no need for you to ask Jesus into your heart." His answer satisfied my inquiry. I just needed to affirm that he was not another judgmental joker.

Josephine and her Mother, Sister Curry, were two women with insatiable appetites. They ate everything on their plates, and when offered more, accepted another generous helping, and when the time came for them to depart to their own homes, they requested "doggy bags."

They committed themselves to come to my home on a weekly basis for Bible teaching and prayer. For the next scheduled Bible study I invited a few of my friends who were members of local churches in our community. Jermaine, a firm Baptist believer and long time school teacher, was an enthusiastic student of the word of God. Charles, and his fiancé' Grace, were devout Catholics.

The Smiths seemed to be quite pleased that there were other invited guests. During this teaching session Elder Smith taught again from the book of Romans, covering the topics of salvation, justification, and condemnation. After teaching, Elder Smith opened the floor for questions. He was bombarded with questions. One concerned the teaching of mediators between God and us. Elder Smith answered that question by taking us to the Bible, showing us in Hebrews that there is one mediator, Jesus Christ. Charles and Grace questioned him on habits smoking, drinking, fornication. Again Elder Smith brought us to the answers that the Bible teaches, no speculation, no judgment, nothing but the uncorrupted Word of God.

When all questions were answered, Mother Curry began singing an old song of the church, " I Need Thee Oh I Need Thee," as Elder Smith began to anoint our foreheads with olive oil. He prayed for each of us in turn. When my turn came to be prayed for, an unusual feeling came upon me. I began to scream out loud, and I fell backwards on the floor. While on the floor, I felt my body twist, and heard my voice screaming, but I had no control to stop the hollering or the twisting. Elder Smith bent over me and whispered in my ear, "There is an unclean spirit (demon) that the Lord is delivering you from, just follow my instructions." It was one of the most unusual experiences that I've ever had in my life. I was aware of everyone in the room. However it was if I was under the control of something or someone else. Elder Smith said, "Relax, I will speak to this spirit and command it to come out of you and never to return again." Elder Smith began calling out names such as: nicotine, lust, lying, pride, fear, hopelessness, hurt. After each name that was called my body would involuntarily twist, accompanied by my screaming and crying. Then just when it seemed this experience would never end, Peace. Peace like I have never known before, Peace that engulfed my very soul. Peace that grasped me in my mind and I knew instinctively that I would be all right. I was so calm, abundant in serenity, all of the anger I had harbored for so many years towards my ex-husband was gone. The resentment I felt having to raise my children as a single parent—gone. I loved everyone, there was no space in me for resentment, hate or retaliation. Even my co-workers at the New Orleans Police Department, towards whom in the past I'd felt some ire, now because of this completely overwhelming peace, they were forgiven. It really did not make sense to harbor any further anger or resentment.

Jermaine, Charles, and Grace were gone by the time I came to myself. I had this wonderfully happy, peaceful feeling all over my entire body. I was sweaty, tired, did not know what had gone on, but was fully content. Elder Smith told me that the Lord had gloriously delivered me from several unclean spirits. He then explained to me that since I had been delivered, I could pray and ask the Lord Jesus Christ to fill me with His precious Holy Ghost. I said, "I don't know what or who you are talking about when you say Holy Ghost, but if it feels anything like I feel now, I want it." He laid his hand on my forehead and began to pray and ask Jesus to fill me with the Holy Ghost with the evidence of speaking in tongues. Josephine and Sister Curry all surrounded me in prayer. They encouraged me to say thank you Jesus, over and over again.

As I began to thank the Lord, this unintelligent, unknown, unlearned sound came forth from my mouth. The more I allowed this language to come forth, the better I felt. When the Smiths left the house, I attempted to say goodbye to them as they were leaving. I intended to ask questions about what I was experiencing. However, the only words in English that proceeded from my mouth were, "What is... is this...?" The rest of my words were interrupted by the flow of some other language, that I couldn't understand. Somehow the Smiths understood, smiled and said, "We will call you tomorrow on the telephone and talk with you." When they left Sarah sat on the sofa and began to thank the Lord Jesus Christ for filling me with HIS precious Holy Ghost with the evidence of speaking in tongues. She prayed for me, my children, my walk with Jesus, the specific plan, and place that HE had called me to, and that I might stand in the midst of uncertainty, adversity, unpredictable changes, and persecution. As she prayed I listened intently, and held her words in my heart. Little did I know that the uncertainty, unpredictable changes, and persecution would arrive all too soon.

The next day Elder Smith called to confirm what Sarah had already explained, that I had been baptized in the Holy Spirit as evidenced by my speaking in tongues. My initial response was "I have never experienced anything like that before in my entire life." Laughing, he said, that Jesus in the Holy Ghost was with me for the rest of my life. I had so many questions. "What am I to do now? Am I supposed to stop wearing make up like Josephine and Sister Curry? Am I never to wear slacks again"? "Basically, he said, Jesus desires for you to share your faith in HIM and your baptism experience in the Holy Ghost with others, and as I continue teaching the Word of God at our Bible Studies, HE will answer all your questions through HIS Word".

As our Bible studies progressed, Elder Smith taught us through the Word of God how to pray, and develop trust and dependency in the Lord. The Bible study participation grew to eleven persons—Sarah, Cindy, Jermaine, Charles and Grace, my five children, and I to sixteen in three weeks. Unfortunately, I attributed the growth to people who wanted to know more about Jesus and us sharing our new found faith and experiences with other church members. The growth came out of Jermaine, Charles, Grace, and myself sharing our faith and experiences in the home Bible study with our local Pastors and congregation.

Inevitably, Charles and Grace were baptized in the Holy Ghost, evidenced by the manifestation of their speaking in tongues. Jermaine's position was as her Pastor had taught her, was that she received the Holy Ghost when she accepted Jesus Christ, therefore she did not have to experience tongues. Her Pastor sent one of the deacons from their church to join in the Bible study to find out about the false doctrine that was being taught. Deacon Leroy was a very personable man, very humble and unassuming. He was a respected God-fearing man in the church as well as in the community. No one suspected that he had been sent by Jermaine's Pastor. He listened very intently as the lessons were taught from the Bible.

One evening as Elder Smith finished his teaching and was about to pray for the entire group, Deacon Leroy interrupted. "Elder Smith, I have something to say." Elder Smith motioned for him to take the floor. "Elder Smith, I must confess that I initially started attending these Bible studies because my Pastor had requested me to investigate the teaching that was going forth. I shared my findings with our Pastor, advising him that the teachings were consistent with the Bible. I want to apologize to you, your wife and mother-in-law, and more to Sister Pansy, because you welcomed me into your home as a guest and I accepted. What you did not know is that I had a hidden agenda, please forgive me. Elder Smith, will you lay your hands on me that I might receive the baptism of the Holy Ghost?" My response was, "Deacon Leroy you are forgiven."

Everyone at the Bible study was both shocked and elated. Shocked that Jermaine's Pastor would stoop so low. Elated that Deacon Leroy was so convinced of the truth that he made a decision to receive the Holy Spirit. Jermaine appeared to be embarrassed by Deacon Leroy's confession. Nevertheless, we all gathered in a circle around Deacon Leroy and Elder Smith. Elder Smith anointed Deacon Leroy's head with olive oil, and requested all of us to pray to the Lord Jesus Christ that HE would fill him with the Holy Spirit. Shouts of Hallelujah, Praise the Lord, filled the room as we all prayed together. After about fifteen minutes, sure enough, Deacon Leroy began to speak in tongues. He shouted, "Hallelujah! Thank you Jesus!" in a language we all understood as we rejoiced with him.

In between his praises in English came forth a beautiful language that none of us had ever heard, or could understand. Suddenly Deacon Leroy began to speak out real loud with unquestionable words that encouraged us to continue praying and, he said, "I am well pleased with you MY children, do not to be distracted, nor discouraged by the contradictions of men, but to believe in ME, praise ME, obey ME, serve ME, and talk to ME daily in prayer." Everyone was quiet. I had no idea what that speech from Deacon Leroy was all about. Nothing like this had ever happened in our Bible studies before. We remained quiet while Deacon Leroy continued to praise the Lord. When Deacon Leroy quieted down, the room grew more quieter and peaceful. It was like a lingering presence of peace was still with us, and no one dared to speak. Just to bask in this presence was an experience that I did not want to end.

As I enjoyed this serenity, thoughts began to come into my mind. I distinctively, heard that Elder Smith, would be traveling to Jamaica, not Haiti, for his next missionary tour. I also heard this voice tell me that Deacon Leroy would Pastor a small church on the outskirts of New Orleans. As we continued resting in this serene atmosphere, Elder Smith spoke out. "The Lord is speaking to someone and wants that person to tell the entire group what HE is saying to them in their thoughts!" Silence continued. I heard the voice again very clearly, very gently, without urgency, permeating my mind to speak the things that HE had placed in my thoughts.

Involuntarily, my body began to shake uncontrollably. The room remained quiet and calm, but even with closed eyes, I could feel someone standing in front of me. Quickly, I opened my eyes, and right in front of me was Elder Smith. He grasped my hand in his and began to pray, "Father, loose her from her fears and let YOUR words flow from her mouth in Jesus' name. Amen." Immediately, I began to tell Elder Smith what I had heard this voice saying to me, that his next missionary trip would be to Jamaica, not Haiti. Crying, I stepped back to sit on the couch.

I loved the Lord so much I did not desire to be dis-obedient to HIM, but I was afraid to speak out, thinking that those thoughts that I heard were my own thoughts. Elder Smith walked to me as I sat on the couch, and he was crying too. He said, "You did not know that those two places have been areas that I have been seeking GOD for specific directives as to where HE desired me to go. Today, GOD has answered my prayers, and confirmed HIS word through the word of knowledge. My dear, I believe there is still a word from the Lord that HE desires to speak to us. Everyone, pray that God will speak to HIS people." I wondered if I was to tell Deacon Leroy about him eventually becoming a Pastor. Instead of speaking forth that word I entered into prayer with the rest of the Bible study participants. Jermaine began to speak, and said, "I just hear in my mind that Deacon Leroy will be a pastor in the future, possibly outside New Orleans." I was absolutely amazed! My mouth fell open in complete surprise! The expression on my face must have changed radically because, Elder Smith asked me, "What is wrong?" Stammering, I said, Nothing is wrong, but you will not believe that I had the same thought, and an additional thought that Deacon Leroy's church will be located on the outskirts of New Orleans." The rest of the people in attendance at the Bible study were just as amazed as I was. We were all perplexed at the events that had taken place. I fully understood why Deacon Leroy spoke in tongues, but the words that Deacon Leroy spoke, as if he was speaking in GOD'S place were suspicious. I fully understood that Deacon Leroy's initial speaking was an experience like I had being filled with the Holy Ghost. But it was his speaking and interpreting what he spoke that cast shadows of doubt in my mind. All of these things were totally new to me. The word of knowledge coming to me in thoughts and when I failed to speak out what I heard in my mind, the exact same thing was spoken by Jermaine! This was truly mind boggling!

Even the validity of my experience was all very new, disconcerting, and puzzling. As I observed the other participants in the room, from the expressions on their faces, their minds were thinking what is this? When the presence of peace lifted from us, we still had many questions. Instead of answering our questions as we presented them, Elder Smith instructed us to take our Bibles and turn to the Book of Acts. Applying Biblical scriptures, he explained the exceptional experience we had witnessed. Personally, my excitement level exceeded anything that had ever happened to me before. Just to think about the GOD of creation, the Creator of everything seen and unseen, had used me to speak to HIS people, I was astonished. My self-esteem went up one thousand percent.

I was finally accepted. HE knew everything about me, yet still loved me, and is using me to give HIS people words. That one experience with the HOLY SPIRIT gave me such a sensitivity to listen for HIS words. I began to have conversations with HIM. I would speak in tongues and then I'd hear my own voice begin to speak in English, an interpretation of the words I had previously spoken in tongues. Miraculously, I knew things about people, their illness, family concerns, directions that they were struggling with, that under ordinary circumstances without the HOLY SPIRIT, I would not have known.

Whenever our Bible group got together, the HOLY SPIRIT would instruct me to lay hands on certain individuals and to pray for them. In obedience, I would lay my hands on their heads, and they would drop to the floor as if they had fainted. I began to have dreams and visions that would actually come true.

Excited about the events that were happening in my life with Jesus, I decided to schedule an appointment with my Pastor, Reverend Lowell, to advise him of all the wonderful things that had been happening in our Bible study, and to request him to guide me, as it was obvious to me that I would be in some sort of leadership role in the church. On the day of my appointment, I arrived fifteen minutes early. I was still thrilled about all of the manifestations of the HOLY SPIRIT operating in my life. The voice of Gloria, Rev. Lowell's secretary interrupted my preoccupation. "Rev. Lowell is ready to see you."

Rev. Lowell's office was huge. He sat at a large dark mahogany desk, in a brown leather chair, surrounded by bookcases. On one side of the room were certificates and degrees hung neatly on the wall. On the other side of the room there were pictures of the Pastor, his wife, and children. Cordially, the Pastor invited me to have a seat. Rev. Lowell was a seminary-trained man with a Doctorate degree in Theology. His sermons were so profound, that they went over most of the congregation's heads, including mine. He was a tall, slender man about in his mid-fifties. While taking my seat, I began hurriedly to tell Rev. Lowell about all the events that had taken place since the inception of the Bible study. He looked at me rather quizzically, but I continued on. I told him how Jermaine's Pastor had sent Deacon Leroy to spy on us and how Deacon Leroy started speaking in tongues as he was prayed for by Elder Smith. I did not leave out one word or occurrence, even explaining my introduction to Elder Smith and his family.

Finally I completed everything I thought I should tell him. Then Rev. Lowell said, "Is this the reason for this meeting?" "No," I answered, the purpose that I requested this meeting was to ask for your assistance in either mentoring me, recommending me to a school, as it is obvious to me that I need more instruction in order to properly exercise myself in the church."

Rev. Lowell's brows wrinkled. Pyramiding his hands, he swirled in his chair with his back to me. "An ecclesiastical associate of mine advised me of the Bible study, as well as the other false teaching and doctrine that is taking place in your home. My concern as your Pastor is that you are being swayed into some type of cult. My advice to you is to discontinue this home Bible study nonsense and attend the Wednesday night teachings and prayer at your own church!" Turning his chair around to face me he said, "As to answer your questions about Bible study, referring you to a class, or the remote possibility of my mentoring you is absurd, you are so polluted with false doctrine, I doubt if the Lord HIMSELF could get you straightened out!"

I was astonished, and righteously angry. My response to my Pastor came off as quiet and calm, even though inside I was furious. "It amazes me that you never asked me about what was being taught in the Bible studies. You took someone else's word who have never attended the studies, you believed hearsay. I am quite surprised that a man of God with your intellectual abilities would come to an illogical decision, without first hearing all the facts". As I got up from my seat, Pastor Lowell said, "I will continue to pray for you that the Lord doesn't send the whole group to hell!" Walking out of his office door, I turned and responded, "God does not send people to hell, Pastor, people make dumb choices based on ignorance, just as you have done."

As I slammed the door behind me, Gloria looked at me as I fumed past her. Hurriedly, she got up from her desk to escort me out. She asked, "Are you OK? What is the problem? Maybe I can be of some assistance?" With the palm of my hand facing her, my body language spoke real loud, leave me alone, this is not the right time to talk to me!

As I walked around the corner to my house all I could think of was how shocked I was to get that type of response from Pastor Lowell. I was even more upset by his inferring that God would send the entire Bible class to Hell.

I considered leaving the church that I had been a member of for the last twenty years. The more I thought about leaving, the more convincing the option appeared. That experience was my first encounter with the different denominational doctrines and the ongoing fights that ensued from this division in creeds. Unfortunately, it was not my only experience with divisions, dogmatism, and defamation in the local churches. In later years I would struggle with these issues again.

As I grew in the knowledge that God has a specific purpose and plan for every individual's life, it was not long before I knew what ministry gift I was given. One of the gifts that operated in my life was prophecy—foretelling and speaking forth the Word of God. My premature interpretation of this gift was that I had been called to preach the word of God. In the church circles that I traveled, this was not the most acceptable calling for a woman.

In the sixties many of the local bodies of believers experience what was then called the "Charismatic Movement." This movement was so named because many untraditional churches and their parishioners began to experience speaking in tongues, interpretation of tongues, and healings. Words of wisdom and knowledge began to come forth from parishioners, who had no teaching or experience with this phenomenon. It was a strong witness to the teachings in the Bible, as recorded in the Book of Acts, after the resurrection and ascension of Jesus. These events changed and upset many common church beliefs.

During the early seventies, the church went through a reformation. The issue of women being called to preach the gospel, or even stand in the pulpit was still being debated. However, some non denominational churches fully embraced the women, while the traditional churches remained rigid in their unacceptance of women in ministry. This unacceptance of women in ministry, resulted in many parishioners leaving their traditional churches, and joining churches with more liberal beliefs. Now to add fuel to the fire, here I was a female called to bring forth the word in a male dominated vocation. During these times, the women in churches were either in the choir, ushers, deaconesses, or recording/financial secretaries. It was considered acceptable for females to cook, clean, and serve meals in the church, but it was unheard of in our church circles that a female was called to preach the word of God. When I began to realize the prompting of the Holy Ghost confirming my gift and calling, I would not share this calling with anyone, especially those who were members of Rev. Lowell's church.

Elder Smith and his wife and mother-in-law had left for Haiti, and I was alone, with no one to talk this over with. Going to Rev. Lowell was out of the question, as I already knew his stance on many of the beliefs I embraced. Having no one to relate to, I was left to communicate with the Lord Jesus Christ. In my infantile state, there were many times I thought the Holy Spirit was speaking to me, and due to my lack of scriptural knowledge (The Word of God), I made many errors. Errors in judgment, errors in speaking forth words that were not supported by the word of God. Enthusiastic, passionate, excited, about the call of God on my life? Yes, but not a practitioner of witchcraft, nor a corrupt person, as I would later be called. This type of narrow mindedness was the result of bigotry in the church.

There were times that I longed for human companion-ship, someone who would understand what I was going through and who could help me to understand what God was doing in my life. Instead of loving, compassionate support from the church leaders and members, I was the recipient of rejection, persecution, dogmatism and defamation. Defamation came as a result of an incident that occurred in church after choir rehearsal. Normally, after choir we all went to our respective homes. However this was a special occasion. We were to share in Louise's birthday celebration. Louise sang lead alto in the choir. She was a very charming lady who was celebrating her thirtieth birthday, and wanted to share cake, ice cream, and other goodies with her fellow choir members. We waited around the kitchen area as other choir members prepared to set up the food that had been graciously prepared for us. We all wanted to sing happy birthday to her and to have her open her gifts. While we waited, without warning, Sis. Riley fell to the floor in what appeared to be a faint. Someone yelled, "Get a cold towel!" As the crowd gathered around Sis. Riley, one of the other choir members suggested, "We had better call an ambulance!" As the cold compress was applied to Sis. Riley's head, her eyes fluttered open and rolled back in her head. Someone yelled, Did anyone call for an ambulance?" The response was, "The police said that an ambulance has been dispatched."

Pastor Lowell was attempting to get Sis. Riley's attention by calling out her name, "Laura, Laura, the ambulance is on the way! Just be still, and you will be all right!" As Sis Riley's eyes began to flutter open, I could tell something was wrong! I heard animal sounds growling come forth from deep within her, as her eyes rolled back in her head! Pastor Lowell looked a bit frightened, and summoned his niece Lou, to come and stay with her until the ambulance arrived. I continued to hear low pitched growls, screams, and a very deep voice clearly stating "I hate Jesus, I hate Jesus!" At this time everyone in the room became very fearful and alarmed. Some of the choir members began to leave the church for fear of what was transpiring before the eyes of everyone present. Sis. Riley lay on the floor;

her face became contorted, and her eyes were spinning in her head. Pastor Lowell again made a feeble attempt to soothe the people as panic and fear swept the entire room. As I continued to stare at this strange materialization, distinctly I heard the Holy Spirit say to me "Cast him out!" My thoughts whirled in my head, immediately I began to reason to myself. I know this is not God telling me to cast out a demonic spirit in the midst of all these people, who know nothing of unclean spirits! Again, the Holy Spirit said, "Cast him out, this is a demon, use the authority that is in the name of Jesus!" In the distance I could hear the sirens as they approached the church. My body shook uncontrollably, as I stepped forth to kneel and obey the Holy Ghost. As I entered the middle of the circle where Sis. Riley was lying, it was my intention to whisper in her ear and command the unclean spirit to leave her in the name of Jesus. However, this was not the intention of the Holy Ghost. As I stooped down, I felt a hand on my elbow. As I turned it was Pastor Lowell physically pulling me away. "Sister there is nothing that you can do, give Sis. Riley some space so that's he can breathe!" While pulling my arm away from his grip, I said "There is nothing that any of us can do, but Jesus can and will do something!" As I began to stoop down again, this loud voice came forth from me saying, "IN THE NAME OF JESUS CHRIST, SATAN I COMMAND YOU TO COME OUT OF THIS WOMAN, NOW!" Immediately the room grew quiet as Sis Riley, again passed out. "Get out of here you witch," Pastor Lowell commanded. "You have caused this woman to have a heart attack." All of the choir members began to look at me skeptically. Unfrightened by their stares, I repeated the command, "COME OUT OF THIS WOMAN IN THE NAME OF JESUS CHRIST!" By this time the paramedics had arrived and everyone was making room for them to come into the dining hall of the church. Again, I commanded the unclean spirit to depart from this woman and not to ever return in Jesus' name. Without warning, Sister Riley sat up and began to praise God with a loud voice, saying, "Thank you Jesus over and over again. As the paramedics reached Sis. Riley she was still praising God, while they attempted to get information concerning her medical history.

"Madame, are you currently taking any medications?"

"Thank you, Jesus, no I am not, but I'm feeling fine, I don't need to go with you to see the doctor."

Madame, we will need to take your vital signs and call all this information into the emergency room, and the doctors at the hospital will make a determination as to whether we are to transport you to the emergency room."

Sis Riley got up off the floor where she had been seated, and said, "Dr. Jesus is using Sis Pansy, and has already healed whatever was wrong with me. I don't believe your doctors could have done what HE has done, I am going home!"

Rev. Lowell interrupted, "Sis, you had better do what these men suggest, they know what is best."

"They only know what the schools have taught them, my Lord Jesus Christ has healed me, and that is that."

Rev. Lowell said, "Sis, this could make you very sick and possibly your condition could worsen."

Brushing her clothing off, Sis Riley looked at Rev. Lowell and said, "I don't mean to disrespect you, but I am healed, the Lord used Sis. Pansy, and HE healed my body, and I ain't going to the hospital, and that's final."

With those words she turned to me and said "You continue to obey GOD, and not man, thank you Jesus," and walked out of the church leaving us all confounded. The ambulance driver yelled after Sis. Riley, "We will not be responsible for you if you walk away refusing medical attention!" But she had left the church, and I do not know if she heard him or cared to hear him. Everyone was amazed.

The choir members left in the dining hall began to gather in groups and talk about what had just happened. The incident that had just transpired was baffling. They whispered staring and snickering amongst themselves. I perceived that I should leave, I turned to walk towards the door, and all of a sudden, Rev. Lowell said, "This is a direct result of people being involved with false teachings, witches, and witchcraft! Sis. Pansy is a witch, teaches false doctrines, and practices witchcraft!" I was stunned, shocked, and shamed. Stunned, because Rev. Lowell's statement was totally confusing, my head reeled with disbelief at what I had just heard. Shocked and offended, that if he thought these things of me, perhaps he should have handled it differently. Even to teach the congregation on demon possession would have been a breech in his denominational doctrine. Indignant and down right angry that he would have the unmitigated gall to say them in public. When in fact, his teaching to the congregation was that demons did not exist except in the minds of unlearned men. Shamed, because of the accusations that he had made in front of my friends. Rev. Lowell was considered a man of God and a pillar of the church. If he made this type of public slander in front of the church, the accused person was shunned, forsaken, and ill treated as though they had the plague. Tears welling up in my eyes, I walked towards the door without dignifying his accusations with a response. I was so hurt that I cried all the way home, wondering what I had done that was wrong. I only obeyed what the Holy Spirit told me to do. When I reached home, I opened the front door and was greeted by my children. They noticed my tear-stained face and became very concerned about me. "What happened, Mom? What is the matter? Are you all right?" Quickly, I went to the bathroom to wash my face. They all huddled around the bath-room door, curious little faces peering at me. After regaining my composure I told my children "I'm fine, Pastor, said some-thing very disturbing to me, and it really hurt my feelings, but I am okay." Jambila the two year old said, "Pastah is a bad man, he made Mom cry, we don't go to his church no more, right Mom?" "Right baby, we will not set foot in his church again." All of my children laughed, as I hustled them off to bed.

Sarah and Cindy had gone to bed early, because Sarah had an early morning appointment for Cindy at the doctor's office. Finally, after taking a long leisurely bath, I retired to bed. I spent my time in the bathtub thinking about what had happened. Attempting to relax in the hot water was futile. Back in my room, I got on my knees to pray, I could not stop the tears from flowing from my eyes. I guess my prayers were just as incoherent to God as they were to me. It relieved me a lot to know that HE knows. The last time I remembered glancing at the clock it was 4:22 AM.

The ringing of the telephone awakened me at 7:00 AM. Gloria, Pastor Lowell's secretary, was on the other end of the line. "Hello, this is Gloria, girl what happened last night at choir rehearsal?" "Gloria, I am still sleepy, I had a very difficult time getting to sleep last night." She persisted, "I heard that Sis Riley got sick and you healed her!" By this time I was becoming suspicious and aggravated. Suspicious of Gloria's calling me, because she worked at the church for Rev. Lowell; aggravated that she insisted on talking to me even though I told her I was tired. My mind ruled out any other motive except, nosiness. I responded, "Gloria, just in case you are calling me and Pastor Lowell is listening on the other line, or you plan to give him a verbatim account of our conversation, save your breath! Don't call me to get an account of what happened last night, ask your boss. And tell him for me, to expect to hear from my attorney for his slanderous accusations!" With those scathing remarks, I slammed the telephone into it's receiver.

All day long I received telephone calls from members of the choir, who either wanted to condemn what Pastor Lowell said to me, or to condemn or condone my actions with Sis. Riley. By the end of the day, I was so angry, and devastated, I only wanted to be alone to console myself. The next day I contacted my attorney to find if I had grounds for a defamation of character lawsuit. Mr. Green, said, "Yes, you do have grounds for a lawsuit, but who would testify on your behalf?" He continued to counsel me over the telephone by saying, "From a Christian perspective, your Pastor was wrong. However, how many people will be hurt, or spiritually hindered as a direct result of this lawsuit should you decide to pursue it? Baby, I know that you are hurt, and angry, but will you promise me that you will pray and allow the Lord to lead you in this very sensitive matter?" Reluctantly, I agreed to not pursue litigation without prayer. Before I hung up, Mr. Green asked me to read I Corinthians, the sixth chapter. As I hung up the telephone, I thought, I do not care to hear another sermon nor to be taught another spiritual principle, I want revenge! My desire was to make this man pay for the pain, embarrassment, and slander that I experienced as a direct result of his verbal assault on my character.

As the days passed, so did my vindictive thoughts of retaliation towards Pastor Lowell. Several weeks later, as I thumbed through some notes I had made to myself, there was the scripture, I Corinthians sixth chapter, that Mr. Green, had given me to read. Reluctantly, I opened the Bible to read the entire sixth chapter of I Corinthians. I was immediately convicted by the words, "Dare any of you having a matter against another go to law before the unrighteous, and not before the saints?" (I Corinthians 6:1NKJV) As I read the entire sixth chapter I realized that had I pursued my lawsuit, I would have been in direct disobedience to the word of God. Right there, without going any further, carrying hostility, unforgiveness, and guilt, I asked the Lord to forgive me. I felt so relieved as I went before the Lord confessing all of my sins and basically emptying myself to HIM, so that HE could fill me up again with HIS Holy Spirit. When Sarah and Cindy returned from the doctor's office, I was in the living room still basking in HIS presence. Sarah asked, "What happened to you, your face is glowing?" "Sarah, sit down, I need to share something with you." I then shared the entire incident that occurred at the church with Sis. Riley, and the scenario that resulted with Pastor Lowell. I told Sarah of all the bitterness, anger, and guilt that I had been harboring. Then I shared with her how the Holy Spirit orchestrated events that I would read the scripture that my attorney suggested, and the resultant conviction and repentance. Sarah replied, "Is that the reason you stopped the Bible study?" "Yes, I was so ashamed and guilty, because of Pastor Lowell's accusation, I felt I could never hold my head up again." Sarah responded, "Girl, I am glad HE worked it out with you, but let's get back to our Bible study". "Sarah, who will teach us? Elder Smith his wife and mother-in-law are gone, are you ready to teach the Bible class? As for me I know that I have a lot more to learn. So without a preacher, we will have to terminate Bible class."

Consequently, one adverse incident in the local church shut down the Bible study, however this incident also drove me into an insatiable search for the things of God. To learn more about HIS word, the Holy Spirit, the gifts of the Spirit, His destiny for my life, HIS design for my life, and my devotion and dedication to HIM became my daily pursuit.

PART THREE

SCENTED FOR SERVICE

And He said to them, "Go into all the world and preach the gospel to every creature. And these signs will follow those who believe, In my name they will cast out demons: they will speak with new tongues:" Mark 16:15,17 NKJV

In The Home

After living over twenty one years in New Orleans after my separation from Larry, I knew that the Lord was calling me to return to California. Los Angeles was the place the Holy Spirit impressed me to reside in. Byron had joined the military, and was living in Maryland. Gerard moved away from home two years after Byron joined the armed forces to find his place and purpose in life. Jasmine and Juleah, decided they would rent an apartment together while attending college and working part time. My children leaving the home so suddenly, and basically all within years of each other, had me going through an "empty nest syndrome." Often while in the process of rearing my children, I'd think, when are they going to grow up and leave? However, when the "branching out" process began in my home, emotionally I was unprepared. If anyone would have told me that I'd miss being the supporter, mediator of sibling arguments, emotional adviser for lovebirds/decision maker, teacher/chief cook/ chauffeur/tutor/teacher/dishwasher/laundrywoman/and maid I would have responded, "I'll miss that as much as I miss a migraine headache!" But I did miss wearing all those hectic hats.

Sarah and Cindy moved into their own apartment. Cindy had bonded with my children and they called her, "their other little sister." Cindy cried as Sarah packed their clothing and belongings. She cried so much that her crying became contagious, and my kids, Sarah, and I all were crying. It wasn't like we would never see them again, they were only moving a fifteen minute bus ride away from our house. I was crying because most of my children were leaving the nest, and I was also losing a friend.

During the three years that Sarah and Cindy had lived with us, we talked a lot. I believe our sharing a lot of intimate details regarding the things we had been through was therapeutic for both of us. Eventually, Sarah was hired by the school system as an elementary school teacher, and I was hired as a Social Worker with a local community agency. Sarah and I had made an agreement for her to pay a small portion to me each month, and she would purchase food for herself and Cindy. We had learned to live with each other quite harmoniously, and now I would be left alone, just Jambila and I.

Jambila was twelve years old, and learning too swiftly how to cleave to her peers and not to her Mom. This type of behavior was normal for a twelve year old. However, my emotional state was such that I viewed this bonding with her peers as betrayal and abandonment. When I told my children, I was moving, to California, they wanted me to stay in New Orleans. I explained to the best of my ability the calling that was on my life. I was under directions and command by the Holy Spirit. After the kids got over the initial shock of Jambila and I relocating to Los Angeles, they participated in the selling of the household goods, and became enthusiastic about visiting with Jambila and me in California.

The church family we had settled into was encouraging and supportive. The Pastor and congregation raised an offering for Jambila and myself to assist us in defraying the costs of relocation. I'll never forget how emotionally draining it was for me the night that Jambila and I were to start out on our relocation to Los Angeles.

Some of my friends decided they would throw a going away party. Even though it was a sweet, great idea, I was not too enthusiastic about it, because of the emotional strain that I would inevitably have to deal with. I wanted to load the car with luggage, say goodbye to my family, and start my driving trip to California with eyes not blurred by tears. Nevertheless, to appease my friends, I consented to the going away party. People started gathering around 7 PM, they brought gifts, food, and well wishes. As the party came to an end the guests decided they would pray for Jambila and myself. They prayed for safe traveling, prosperity, and for God's purpose and plan to be fulfilled in all my ways. As the guests said their good-byes, one sister who very rarely said anything, came to me for a hug. As we were hugging she spoke in my ear saying "Sister, the Lord will use you in the place where you are going mightily in extrication of demonic spirits." She further exhorted me to maintain a close relationship with the Lord in prayer and fasting so that I would hear HIM and obey HIM. Well, that was not a word that I was thrilled about receiving. No wonder this sister was quiet! When she said something like this, who would believe that it came from the Lord? Certainly not me. This casting out demon stuff was in essence the very thing that had got me in trouble with the church leadership, I thought. Was she ever off! I politely thanked her and quickly dismissed any thoughts of me fulfilling those words. I did not fully understand all of God's purpose regarding my going to Los Angeles, but I fully understood that it was not for the purpose that this dear sister had just said. I knew that God's purpose for me was to serve, but to send me into the very thing that had caused me to be blackballed from my church was too inconceivable for me to comprehend.

As the last guest departed, I closed the door, and told Jambila that we would be leaving in about an hour. Thankful that we had packed the automobile earlier in the day, I settled down across the bed just to do a mental check that I was not forgetting anything. Exhausted from the packing, I must have fallen asleep because the knocking on the front door startled me. I wondered who can this be? Mary, a fellow minister, greeted me, by saying "I'm sorry to disturb you but I could not get any rest knowing that I had not obeyed God in what HE told me to do." In my mind I wondered OK what now? Mary was a full figured, strikingly beautiful younger woman who had been mentored by another female Pastor who had gone home to be with the Lord. Most of this deceased Pastor's members seemed to be unable to bond in any other ministry. Mary and I had become acquainted, and we had a lot in common. Both of us were called to preach, both of us were pleasingly plump, and we both were prayer warriors in the intercessory prayer group at church. Mary continued, " I heard the Holy Spirit tell me to offer to assist you in the drive to Los Angeles." "How will you get back to New Orleans Mary?," I asked. I knew that Mary was currently unemployed, her Dad was terminally ill in San Francisco, and she wanted to see him so that she could offer him the opportunity to accept Jesus. Mary answered, " I have a few dollars that I could eat on en route to Los Angeles, other than that the Lord will provide."

I was elated to know that I would have a companion on the long laborious drive to Los Angeles. Laborious cannot begin to describe our relocation drive. First, the automobile which had been thoroughly checked from top to bottom by my mechanic, began to stop as soon as we turned on the radio. The mechanic in a service station in a little town west of Austin, Texas informed us that the alternator needed to be replaced, and not to play the radio nor to turn the headlights on because the car would automatically turn off. Thus no night driving was possible.My thoughts as we pulled out of the service station were, we can still do this. At some point in our journey I asked Mary to take the wheel because I was exhausted. "Mary, do you have your driver's license?" "No, but I can drive!" Without saying one word I just looked at her, I'm sure rather strangely. "Mary, I thought you were coming along on this trip to assist me with the driving?" "Yeah, that is right, but my driver's license is expired!" I opted to hold back the sarcastic remarks that should have followed these absurd declarations, and quietly said that I would drive the entire trip. At this point one would not have needed spiritual discernment to figure out that I was upset. I was thinking what in the world are you riding with us for? A trip to the West Coast?

Jambila was great company, she chattered every moment she was awake. We drove all day until it was time to eat. It was necessary to have the battery recharged, while we were eating so that the car, a 1980 Rambler station wagon would start. As night began to fall, we would find an inexpensive clean hotel, eat dinner and then, drive the car to the nearest service station so that the battery would be charged by morning. It took us almost four days to motor from New Orleans to Los Angeles.

As soon as we crossed the California border, I telephoned Kinsey. Kinsey was a friend I'd made while I lived in New Orleans. We met at a conference hosted by our home church. I mentioned to her at that time that I heard the Holy Spirit giving me directives to move to Los Angeles. Kinsey told me that she lived with her Mom and sister. She said, "Whenever you decide to obey God, a place for you and your daughter will not be a major concern for you. You are welcome to stay with us until you find employment and housing". So seven months later, Jambila and I were en route to Los Angeles. Kinsey gave me excellent instructions, and we arrived in Los Angeles around 3:00 PM, the week prior to Thanksgiving 1986.

When we arrived, I introduced Mary to Kinsey. Then we proceeded to unload the car. Kinsey interrupted, "You guys don't have to unload the car you will only be here until my sister Chris comes home from work, and you can stay at Chris' apartment." Kinsey's unit had three bedrooms, living room, dining room, kitchen, bath and a bonus room. Kinsey shared this unit with her younger sister, mother, and her son.

Exhausted after a long drive, I just wanted to have a hot bath, settle down between some clean sheets, and sleep. The drive over to Chris' house was short. We took a route that led us onto Wilshire Boulevard. As I observed the tall office buildings, I wondered if I would find employment in one of these places.

Jambila was impressed by the many different kinds of people that lived in Los Angeles. Her experience with different cultures was limited to her white teachers in New Orleans. Before we left New Orleans, she did have an opportunity to know a little about the Vietnamese culture, but only for a short period of time. She informed me that most of the Vietnamese people and their families had to learn to speak English, so she had very little interaction with the students. I considered this an ideal time to tell her about the numerous cultures that resided in Los Angeles.

Strangely, Jambila began to cry. As I attempted to comfort her and to find out the reason for the tears, she said," I do not like it here, I have no friends!" It was at this point I realized that I had become so wrapped up in the inevitable move, that I had not taken the time to find out about her feelings at all. After apologizing to her about my obvious oversight of the friends she left in New Orleans, I began to explain how this relocation was necessary for me to obey the Holy Spirit's directives for my life. Through tears and sobs, Jambila resigned herself to my leadership as her parent. From that day, I began to pray that the Lord would help her to find Godly friends.

When we got to Chris's apartment complex, Mary, Jambila and I unloaded our luggage and personal items. Chris gathered together a few personal items of her own, and said, "I am going to stay with my mother and sister while you are here. Please help yourselves to whatever I have. Here are the telephone numbers where I can be reached at home and work." "Chris, we need not displace you from your apartment, Mary, Jambila and I can make a bed on the floor so that you will not be uncomfortable." Chris insisted that she and her family had already decided that she would relinquish her apartment to us upon our arrival. That night, as I reflected on the events, I was truly overwhelmed by HIS goodness and kindness. As I drifted into sleep I remember saying a special prayer of thanks for Kinsey's family and their loving kindness to us as strangers.

The Thanksgiving and Christmas holidays were nice. We celebrated with Kinsey's family. My finances were just about exhausted, as I had made a deal with Chris to give her money on her utility bills, in addition to having to purchase the food. Very little money was left towards gift giving. Kinsey's family celebrated Christmas like we were accustomed to in New Orleans. We always enjoyed everything about celebrating the birth of Jesus Christ, the shopping, gift wrapping and most of all the huge feast of every type of imaginable food and drink. Kinsey and her family provided for Jambila's clothing, that she was absolutely thrilled to receive.

The Mayes family gave Mary an airline ticket to San Francisco to visit with her dad. My Christmas gift was lingerie, which was beautiful. I received the gifts graciously, however I felt bad that I was not in a position to reciprocate. I think that Kinsey's Mother realized how humbled I felt, and said, "Sister, don't feel bad, God will bless you real soon. We were not always in a financial position to purchase gifts for others, but God has blessed us so therefore we wanted to be a blessing to you. Just remember, when you have an opportunity to be a blessing to some one else, do the same as we have done for you." The words that she spoke pierced my heart and soul. Tears welled up in my eyes and streamed down my face, as I expressed my gratitude for their kindness.

"Thank you so very much, this means a lot to me to know that God has people who loves HIM and HIS people, thank you."

Mary left the next day for San Francisco. Fortunately, the words Kinsey's Mother spoke were not long in being fulfilled. In January of 1987, we moved to our own apartment and I was blessed with employment.

In Samaria

My employment and housing were intimately related, I was a Resident Manager for an apartment complex of 81 units. As the Manager, I was afforded a two bedroom apartment—rent and utility free—as part of my compensation for management duties. When I took over the management responsibilities, the complex had only a twenty five percent occupancy. Only twenty of the units were rented. One of my responsibilities was to rent the apartments to creditworthy applicants, and to bring the occupancy rate up.

My employers were a Jewish Dad and his daughter. Bill had built this eighty-one unit apartment complex for his daughter Terry, as a thirtieth birthday present. Terry was a very pleasant person to know as long as money was not involved. When money came into the relationship with Terry, she transformed into the corrupt, hardened, deranged individual that her Dad, Bill, had trained her to be. As the Resident Manager, it was my charge to report any credit discrepancies to Terry. Based on what I reported to her, she decided what to charge for occupancy.

I observed Terry make heartless decisions to charge prospective residents as much as four times the rent for move-in costs, when the credit report revealed only one adverse entry. On the other hand, I saw her make decisions when the credit report was excellent, to charge the prospective resident two times the rental charge for move-in, when she knew that the person really wanted or needed the apartment. Whenever Terry was not available to report credit discrepancies, I would call Bill, who normally rendered the same type of firm, merciless, insidious penalties. However there were times when I was left alone to use my discretion as to what a prospective resident should pay based on their credit report. It was during these

128

times that I had an opportunity to show the grace and mercy of Jesus Christ. When I would communicate the results of my decision to Terry, she would respond, "You are too easy on these people, you should give them a hard time, make them pay the highest cost that comes into your mind!"

As a newcomer to Los Angeles, it was difficult for me to establish credit, and I needed to purchase living room furniture. Terry decided that my apartment was to be the model apartment for a two bedroom unit. She could transfer my apartment to a revenue-producing unit, by converting it to a model instead of using another vacant apartment. It was her thought that an empty living room in the Manager's unit would not make a great impression on potential tenants. Terry decided to purchase living room furniture for my apartment, and told me that she was giving the furniture to me. I was elated.

We went out to Beverly Hills to select the furniture. The things Terry selected were not my taste; Terry chose contemporary/ modern things. That particular store did not have anything in stock that fulfilled my traditional preference. Terry was annoyed that I did not make a decision on any of the vast stock of furniture that was available at that store. Disgusted she said, "Go to any store you desire and select anything you want, just get some damn decent furniture in that place as soon as possible." With that statement she turned to leave, saying, "Just have the company call me so that your purchase can be placed on my account and do it today! I have an appointment that I cannot miss, so find your furniture, and find it today or I'll revoke my offer to give the furniture to you. I will take the money out of your salary if the furniture is not purchased today!"

Waving good-bye to Terry, I realized that I was faced with a real dilemma. Delighted that the decision to select furniture for my apartment was placed in my hands, but overwhelmed in that I was new to Los Angeles and did not know how to get to the Thomasville outlet in the San Fernando Valley. I called the store and got directions, but I was still afraid that I would get lost and Jambila would come home from school and the door would be locked. She would have no place to stay until I returned home. With fear biting at my heels, I opted to look further in the telephone directory to places that were in Beverly Hills. My knowledge of streets was Wilshire Boulevard, Western Avenue, Olympic Boulevard, and Hauser Bl. Outside these streets I was lost. I found a furniture rental company on Wilshire Boulevard in Beverly Hills.

As I entered the facility I began to browse around the store to see if anything suited my taste in furniture. Walking back to the front of the store, disappointed, because I saw nothing that suited me, I was stopped by a salesperson who asked if he could assist me. I told him that my taste was traditional, and I was looking for living room furniture. Heading towards the front showcase window, he asked, "Have you seen this lovely set that is on display?" In my haste to locate furniture for the living room I had looked past the things that were in the showcase. The sofa was peach with coordinating pillows, there were two green velvet Queen Anne wing chairs, three mahogany tables, a Frederick Cooper lamp, and a mahogany dining room table with four matching chairs. Perfect. The company called Terry to obtain her personal credit information. After spending a little more than two hours in my search to find what I wanted, the transaction was completed and delivery scheduled for the following week.

Communicating effectively with other cultures proved to be a challenge that I could not overcome. However Jambila, made friends very easily with a Korean girl that resided in the same building that I managed. Gina and Jambila were inseparable. When Gina's Dad learned that Jambila and Gina were friendly, he offered her a ride to school. I asked Gina to tell her Dad that we would car pool, he drive one week, and I'd drive the girls the next week. Gina told me that her dad said that would not be necessary, as he had to drive to work and John Burroughs Middle School was down the street from his office.

Gina had to interpret any communication from her dad or grandmother because neither of them spoke much English. Any work order request, to my office, had to be related through Gina. Gina would give any pertinent information to her dad or grandmother in the Korean language. Gina's Mother worked in a local bar and spoke perfect English, however we hardly saw her at all due to the hours she worked and slept. I was never addressed by the Koreans by my name. To the Korean residents, I was "Mon-Knee-jer"—Manager.

Early one morning I was awakened by a small voice at the door, crying out softly, "Mon-knee-jer, Mon-knee-jer!" I rolled over and looked at the clock it was 2:30 AM. Recognizing the little voice as Gina's, I thought, now what in the world could be the matter? Gina's voice persisted, but barely above a whisper, "Mon-knee-jer, Mon-knee-jer," she cried out as she knocked on my apartment door. Agitated, I got out of my bed reached for my robe, and opened the door. Gina stood at the door with a pale tear-soaked face looking at me. "What is the problem Gina? Gina said, my Dad is fighting with my mom, and he has put my mom, grandmother, my little brother and me out of our apartment! Where is your mother? She is upstairs arguing with my Dad. Did you call the police? No, I am afraid if I call the police my Dad will fight me like he is fighting with my Mom!"

Attempting to clear the sleepy haziness from my mind so that I could think rationally, I thought I do not wish to become involved in a domestic dispute. Especially in a domestic dispute where the abuser could not speak English. Not knowing what else to say, I told Gina to tell her Mom that she could call the police from my apartment. Gina left and, as I closed the front door, I could hear a woman screaming upstairs. Gina turned back to me and said, "Mon-knee-jer, I am scared of my Dad, he beats me and my Mom. Gina, you just run upstairs, and tell your Mom that she can use my phone to call the police and I'll be waiting for you here at the door." As I motioned for her to go to her Mom, she looked up at me with big frightened brown eyes and said, "I'll be back!"

Leaving the door partially opened behind Gina, I retrieved my robe from the bedroom. Peering into Jambila's room, I saw that she had not been awakened by Gina's knocking or calling out at the door. Closing Jambila's door to her bedroom, I proceeded back to my front door to wait for Gina's Mom. I wondered, why was I involved with this? Gina's Mom had several neighbors—five Korean families that lived on the second floor, three Korean families on the third floor—that were much closer to where her apartment was located! Why did they have to awaken me at 2:30 AM to settle a domestic dispute? I just wanted to go back to bed and catch up with my sleep!

Soon I could hear a female's voice speaking loudly in the Korean language. Walking outside my door, and looking up, I saw Gina, her little brother, her grandmother, and Gina's Mom Lin. Lin was yelling to the top of her voice back upstairs as she and her family ran downstairs. "Shhhh Lin, you'll wake the entire building up!" They ran past me into my apartment. I was right behind them. As I closed and locked the door, they were already sitting on the floor. My intention was to ask what happened, before I could say anything, Lin, Gina, and the grandmother were already heatedly involved in conversation in their language. Upset that I had been awakened at this hour and they were making enough noise to awaken other families in the building, and indignant that they did not have the common courtesy to speak in a language that I could understand, I yelled, "Hey shut up!" The room grew quiet. Then I asked, "What is the problem?" Lin, began to explain that her husband was an extremely jealous man. She explained that she worked in a club that did not close until 2:00 AM. Whenever he was drunk, he accused her of performing immoral acts with her patrons and her employer. "Lin, you may use the phone to summon the police." I was only slightly interested in what caused the outbreak. I was more interested in this group of people leaving my apartment so that I could resume sleeping. Suddenly, the conversation was interrupted by a knock on the door. Everyone in the room became still, as I moved towards the door. "Who is it? Yung Sung Lee," came back the response. Lin, Gina and the grand mother immediately became agitated. Gina cried, " That's him, that is my Dad! Don't let him in! He will start fighting us again! Pleeeasee Mon-knee-jer don't open the door!" While they were pleading with me, I got out of the chair and went to the door. In the midst of their protestings my mind raced, suppose this man is out of control? Would I be able to handle the situation without it turning into a major disaster? If his English is little and my Korean is none, how will I communicate effectively with him? Is he in such a drunken state that he is unmanageable? Throwing caution to the wind, I opened the front door. Mr. Lee stood at the door bowing repeatedly saying, "Mon-Knee-jer, Mon-knee-jer." I took him by his hand and guided him inside the door. Mr. Lee's breath smelled like a distillery. As I shut the door, Lin, and Gina's grandmother lit into him with an outburst of angry words. I could not understand the language that they spoke, but the spirit was crystal clear.

After hearing several bursts of angry words, I intervened. "Gina, please tell your Daddy for me that he is welcome in my home, but the yelling and screaming has to stop." Gina in her soft, respectful, humble voice translated my request to her Daddy. Mr. Lee again began to bow in a manner that I interpreted as him saying I'm sorry. "Gina, ask your Dad can his wife and mother return to their apartment? If he says yes, tell him to promise me that he will not resume the arguing, and fighting." When Gina spoke to him in Korean, they all began screaming again. "SHUT UP!," I yelled. Gina, tell your Daddy if he continues yelling I will call the police! That goes for you, Lin, and your mother! Mr. Lee again began to bow and said " So sorry Mon-Knee-jer, so sorry"!

Even though I was irritated by being selected as a mediator for a domestic violence dispute, I could not get angry. I thought maybe I'll try another approach. "Gina, ask your Dad does he know Jesus Christ?" As I listened to Gina translate my question, I could tell from Mr. Lee's answers that he was telling Gina about Buddha. Gina told me, "My Dad said that he knows Buddha only! Buddha is his god and he worships and serves him!" Obviously Mr. Lee had heard about Jesus, because he associated his Buddha with my Jesus. Since my attempts to reason with him were fruitless, I decided to use this time to witness to Mr. Lee about Jesus. Gina continued acting as my translator as I compared other gods with Jesus.

I shared through Gina that my Jesus was the only God, and the only One that rose from the dead. I explained that Buddha is an idol that has eyes but cannot see, ears but cannot hear, feet but he cannot walk. As I talked an unusual presence came into that room. I understood it to be the Holy Ghost. I felt HIM, Mr. Lee felt HIM, and began crying. Gina felt HIM and could no longer translate for me as she began to sing in a strange language that was something other than Korean. Lin and her mother-in-law also felt the Presence of the Holy Ghost. "Gina tell your Daddy that what he is feeling is my GOD!" Obediently she stopped singing long enough to tell her Dad in Korean that this presence he was feeling was Mon-knee-jer's GOD! We stayed in this unusual anointing for an extended period of time. It was as if we were caught up in HIS presence and time stood still. I felt my flesh tingling, all tiredness disappeared from me. An incredible peace saturated everyone in the room, no one spoke, we just sat there, we were in total delight.

When the Presence of the LORD lifted, the first person to speak was Mr. Lee. Gina translated what her Dad said to me. "Mon-knee-jer, my Daddy says, Your God is the TRUE GOD!" He turned to his family and spoke a few words in Korean, and they all got up and went to the front door. Just as they went out of the door, Mr. Lee turned and said, "You Jesus for me," and began to bow.

From that morning and during my short time as Manager of those apartments, I never heard a word from Mr. Lee or his family that would even suggest that he was fighting his wife. He continued to transport the girls to school every morning. Whenever I would see him, he'd always bow and say, "Hello Mon-knee-jer".

Having worked in this capacity for five months, the occupancy increased from the initial 25 percent to 98 percent. When the apartment complex occupancy increased to 98 percent, she voiced concerns that I was unable to perform light maintenance duties. Terry also indicated in previous conversations that in her dad's other apartment complexes, they had traditionally hired a husband and wife team. Her next move was to hire someone to act as an assistant Manger. Terry's rationale was that as I ran errands for the complex, no one was on site at the complex. What I did not know was that Terry had hired this woman and her husband to take over my job. In her diabolical, business mind, it was dollar smart for her to hire a couple. This way she had a wife to perform clerical duties and a man to perform maintenance requests, two for the price of one.

My termination was unsuspected. I learned later that this is one of the tools of the trade for apartment owners to lease the building to maximum capacity, and then terminate either the leasing agent or the manager. I was afraid. Here I was with no job, and Terry breathing down my back to vacate the unit. My prolonged stay resulted in my being served with an Unlawful Detainer. The Unlawful Detainer becomes a part of your credit report, thereby alerting future landlords of your past history. Terry was being ruthless, and used this as a tool to rush me out of her building so that her new Managers could take my apartment to live in.

Finally, I was hired by a large company out of Century City to become the Resident Manager of two buildings they had recently acquired. These apartments were located in West Hollywood, California. One unit was largely occupied by students, the other unit was in its final stages of completion and was considered more of a luxury apartment complex. In this capacity, I also obtained experience as a Property Manager. The luxury complex was not quite ready for occupancy, thereby giving me an opportunity to learn about city code requirements necessary prior to the issuing of a certificate of occupancy.

After all code requirements were met, Jambila and I moved to the two-bedroom, two-bathroom manager's unit. Jambila was excited that we were moving to Hollywood. Many nights we'd just walk up and down Hollywood Boulevard's Walk Of Fame. We were like tourists in our new hometown. Together we would go to the local restaurants just about every night instead of cooking meals at home. I think the thing that Jambila enjoyed the most was Mann's Chinese Theater, seeing the hand-and footprints of the movie stars. My personal preference was walking Hollywood Boulevard, and observing the people.

After living in Los Angeles for less than a year, Jambila experienced her first earthquake. The tremors awakened us early in the morning, and we heard screams as the neighbors across the street from our complex exited their building. Jambila and I were scared out of our minds. Jumping out of bed in a sleepy stupor, I ran across the living/dining room area to Jambila's room saying," Are you all right?

Yeah, what was that? I don't know it sounded as though someone ran a car into the wall of the garage." Soon we heard screams, and then banging on the apartment door. "It's an earthquake," someone yelled run for your life! At that point I felt panic overtaking my ability to think logically. Jambila must have felt the same thing because she began to cry and cling closely to me. Making an attempt to reassure her that everything was going to be all right, I sounded doubtful to my own ears. Aftershock after aftershock robbed us of any sleep, we did not know if the building would collapse, or what?

Reluctantly we stayed in our apartment, while our neighbors and the other occupants of our building stayed outside in the park across Sycamore Street. Jambila and I stayed up for the rest of the night, and watched the residents of the building across the street from ours make sleeping arrangements on the ground as though sleeping outside would save them from destruction.

Managing apartments in Hollywood proved to be more of a challenge than I expected. One of my responsibilities as manager was to make daily physical inspections of both properties, and to check for damages, repairs, and vacated units. This particular morning, after opening the leasing office, I walked down the street to the building mostly occupied by young adults attending a music college in Hollywood. The report submitted by the maintenance staff indicated two vacated units. Approaching the building, I opted to take the stairs instead of the elevator to the second floor. Taking this route gave me an opportunity to inspect the common hallways and the laundry facilities. After finding the Master key on my key ring, I opened the door to unit 212. This was a one-bedroom apartment with a balcony. Gathering the clipboard into a writing position, I inspected the entire living room, making annotations for the maintenance crew. Walking to the kitchen, I made a note for the carpet to be shampooed. Opening the pantry, kitchen cabinets, and the refrigerator, also generated notes to the clean up crew. Obviously the residents that moved out were not interested in a refund of their security deposit, I thought. The former occupant vacated the unit and left it in total disorder. Dirty clothing and wet towels were on the floors of both the bedroom and bathroom. These tenants were not delinquent in their rent, I wondered why they had not taken the time to clean up a little. Leisurely walking through the unit making notes, I realized that I had not checked the closet in the bedroom. Feeling for the light switch as I entered the closet I heard a rattling noise. I thought to myself now what in the world could that be? Clothing was scattered all over the closet floor, and the rattling noise was louder. Curious as to what toy was under the clothing, I began to move the clothing about in pursuit of the rattling sound. Suddenly, I overturned an article of clothing and a rattlesnake, coiled up with his rattler extended in the air, appeared! I screamed, dropped the clothing and clipboard and bolted for the door, screaming all the way out of the building. "There is a snake in the building! Do not open your doors! Someone call the police!"

I ran to the corner, opened the gate and went into the office to telephone the police for assistance. After the Police dispatcher kept me on the line, asking, where? Who? When? What color was the snake? Did the snake bite anyone? Why was the snake in the apartment? I understood why the questions needed to be asked but, frustrated, I said, "Please send the Police and alert the Animal Control Unit!"

As Manager it was necessary for me to submit a written report to the owners. I was the one who should have been asking questions. Finally the police arrived with the animal control workers, and removed the snake from the apartment. That experience so shook me up that the entire day was unsettling, and unproductive.

Later that evening the owner of the snake came back to the apartment complex to claim his pet. He came to my office and asked if anyone reported anything unusual in the building. Now the other tenants knew that he had the snake, and that he often purchased live mice and chickens to feed it. My next obvious question to the residents was, "Were you aware that there is a no-pets-allowed clause in the lease? Why was this practice not reported to my office?" Most of them shrugged their shoulders, they said, "We were afraid, and the snake was not harming anyone!"

As the past tenant sat before me looking totally innocent to the infraction of his lease agreement, I decided I'd play the silly game with him. "I'm sorry I have no idea to what you are talking about!" Shuffling his feet, and shifting his weight from one foot to another, looking at the floor. "Well, I heard there was a disturbance in my building this morning in my apartment. Well, Mr. Neal, could the disturbance have possibly been caused because of your pet rattlesnake? Mr. Neal were you not informed by the leasing agent when you rented this apartment, that we have a no-pets-clause?" He shifted his feet and looked up at me stating, "My snake did not harm anyone, and it does not bark and keep others awake at night. My mom said it was all right for me to have Samson to live with me!" Instinctively, I knew that to pursue this conversation would have been fruitless. Hurriedly I decided to complete the process. I obtained a forwarding address, and told him of the location of his pet snake and said, "Farewell and good riddance!"

In Judea

Jambila and I joined a large church in Los Angeles. When we placed our membership with this church it's parishioners numbered over 5000. Soon after completing the new member's class requirement, I joined a class called "The Overcomers." The class proved to be a tremendous blessing in teaching a practical approach to Christian living. Here I learned the true meaning of the words denial of self, deliverance and destiny. I figured I had a running start on the rest of the believers. I had accepted Jesus as my Savior over twenty years ago, been filled with the Holy Ghost for over twenty years, and educated in a Spirit filled college, and taught and preached at several churches in Louisiana and California. I had fed the hungry, clothed the naked, housed the homeless, visited those imprisoned, suffered persecutions and many trials, and was walking in all the knowledge I knew to keep myself unspotted from the world. In other words, I felt I had arrived and knew all about everything there was to know about being a Christian.

It was this type of reasoning that brought me to the conclusion that I needed to do more in aiding others in the body of Christ. My entire focus was that I should be in place where I could be of assistance to someone who could benefit from my experiences. Based on this theory, when I read the church bulletin and saw that there was a need for a Counselor, I applied for the position.

Even though I had been a member of this church for over three years, I only knew the members of my Sunday School class. After applying for the position of Counselor, I wondered did I do the right thing? I remembered that it was my overwhelming drive that had caused me to think that I could make an impact in aiding someone else. I decided that I'd talk to one of the members of the church that had been active in ministry. I needed to get a feel for some of the people that I'd possibly have to work with if the position was offered to me.

After each class was over it was customary for us to exchange warm greetings, say our good-byes, and get extra information regarding church functions. Mother Smith was a seasoned woman of God. According to her testimony she had been a loving wife until her husband died. She had finished rearing her children with the help of the Lord. Mother Smith often told of how miraculously the Lord had provided for her, to support three of her children and send them to college without the benefit of financial aid from the government. Mother Smith was a short, petite woman, that appeared to be about fifty years of age. However, I am sure she was older than that because of the age of her eldest child. She had beautiful silver-gray hair that she kept impeccably cut in a cute style. She supported herself and her children after her husband's death by acquiring several pieces of property and turning them into homes for the elderly.

It was Mother Smith that I chose to talk to. Mother Smith had overcome some mountains in her life, she had weathered some storms, she had come through some trials and tribulations. I did not want to speak to some of the saints that were shallow and unrealistic. I had questions that required real truthful answers.

I approached Mother Smith after class and asked her if I could speak with her. She responded, "Sure". I poured out my heart to her, emphasizing my longing to help people, and the possibility of my obtaining a position on the church staff as a Counselor. I asked her what these people were really like. What would they require of me? " Mother, I want to help!"

Somehow my innermost feeling of wanting to do a significant work for the MASTER must have been conveyed to her. She looked at me with those brown eyes of wisdom, and said, "As to what the people are like, you will have to keep in your sights not to know them according to their flesh, because they have flesh just like you. But you must pray if you intend to stay here and with Jesus. The Lord has already put in you a desire to know HIM, and to be of service to HIS people. If you keep in mind that these are HIS people and you strive to know HIM more, and you'll do well. Your question as to what will they ask you, I don't know. But this I do know, that if the LORD has called you, and desires you to fill this position, HE will give you HIS heart, wisdom, love, and knowledge to love and direct HIS people into a closer relationship with HIM." She closed her conversation with me by praying a very short but effective prayer. "Lord Jesus we pray that YOUR will be done in this situation, and that You will get glory out of the outcome, in Jesus name. Amen."

She hugged me and said, "You are going to be put in a place that the LORD is going to manifest HIMSELF in a greater way to you. Keep praying and thanking HIM for HIS will in your life." As we bid our final good-byes, I admired her and silently thought, I sure wouldn't mind becoming a woman of God like her.

Within the next week I received a telephone call from the Counseling department, informing me of the time, date, and place of the interview for the position of Counselor. I was overcome by a spirit of fear, that constantly told me of my inadequacies, incompetence, and inconsistencies in my walk as a believer. From the time that I got the telephone call until the very day that I stepped across the threshold of the office in the church, the enemy bombarded me with anxiety. The assurance that I once possessed in the initial stages of application soon shadowed under the gloom and doom I was now battling. I fasted and prayed, not for the job nor that the church would choose me, but that the shackles, yokes, and bondage's of fear in me would be destroyed.

Miraculously, as I got out of my car, walked to the church and placed my feet in the office of the Counseling department,

I could feel in my body a freedom that I had not experienced since I had started to pursue the Counseling position. I spoke with a very gracious woman who welcomed me as she obtained my name. She told me to be seated and I would be called momentarily.

Taking a seat in the outer office, I saw that the waiting area was impeccably decorated with fine furnishings, fine artwork, and magazines. The carpet and wallpaper were of coordinating colors of mauve and gray stripes, and tastefully bordered with floral borders at the ceiling and floor. Appreciating all of the beautiful surroundings, and settling my back against the firm upholstered sofa, I dived into one of the office magazines.

Before long my name was called. I was ushered into an office that was even more beautifully decorated than the front office. The gracious woman who escorted me introduced the person who would conduct my interview. She said, "Ms. Hamilton, this is Pansy Bradshaw." Ms. Hamilton shook my hand with a very firm grip while offering me a seat. She opened our interview with prayer. She then proceeded to give me a bit of history of the church and how the Counseling department played an essential part in the in maintenance of spiritual, and psychological well being of the parishioners.

Ms. Hamilton was a well built woman with a noticeably small waistline that was accentuated by a belted dress. Her hair was done in a professional twist with a side bang that covered her ear and hung beneath the chin. Normally I would not have noticed it but somehow this style bothered her. She was constantly brushing her hair from her face with her hand. It appeared that every other word she said she brushed her hair from around her chin, which distracted me and I did not pay much attention to what she was saying. It was when the tone of her voice changed that I realized that Ms. Hamilton had asked me this question for the second time.

"Have you done any counseling before? Have you done any Christian counseling before?

Yes, for a short period of six months I volunteered with the 700 Christian Club in their telephone counseling ministry."

Then she asked, "What principles did you apply in your counseling?"

My answer was, "We were provided with script, as well as a counseling manual that was based upon the word of God."

"Good, I have several tests I will administer to you. First, I want you to provide us with a statement of your personal beliefs, and your personal testimony as it relates to salvation. Then we will administer a written test to evaluate your ministry and motivational gifts in the body of Christ."

For three hours I labored over the narrative portions. It would have been so much simpler, I thought, if she would have asked me questions as opposed to requesting me to write. Over and over I checked for fragmented sentences, spelling, correct punctuation, and continuity. On several occasions Ms. Hamilton's assistant checked to see if I needed anything. Fortunately for me, this was not a time sensitive assignment.

Had it been timed, I'm sure I would have failed miserably. I really desired to do my best, and because it has been a pattern of mine to stress out and make dumb mistakes, I took the time to go over every sentence meticulously.

Finally I finished writing and rang for Ms. Hamilton's assistant to retrieve my papers. When she entered in the room I engaged her in conversation. I said, "I am sorry I took so long to finish, I just wanted to make sure that everything was correct." She answered, My name is Penny, and you have no reason to apologize, I understand. Ms. Hamilton will see you again after she reviews your papers. Would you care for some coffee? If you'd like to stretch your legs for about twenty to thirty minutes feel free to do so. Is there anything that I could get for you? No thank you," I responded as I got up to walk to my car and sit to listen to the radio.

After sitting and unwinding for a few moments, I decided to walk across the street to the restaurant and buy a lemonade. I looked at my watch to see if I still had time. Sipping on a lemonade drink, I enjoyed a typical sunny Southern California day. I thought on my life since I relocated from New Orleans to Los Angeles, California. I thought of every adverse situation that I had been faced with, and how the Lord brought me through each one victoriously.

Even in the relocation process, I was challenged driving from New Orleans to Los Angeles with an automobile that had a defective alternator. Then after arriving in Los Angeles and being blessed with employment and housing, I was terminated. The Lord blessed me with another job in the same field with an increase in wages. I decided that this was not the place that I desired to live or work in long term. The Lord provided a place for Jambila and me to live and HE provided for us all throughout my unemployment. I began praising the Lord for HE alone could do these things. I was so grateful for HIS blessings to us. Looking at my watch, I realized that it was time for me to return to the Counseling department.

As I walked across the street I could hardly contain myself as the praises began to roll up from my belly. I praised HIM out loud, saying HALLELUJAH! I composed myself as I rang the bell. Penny greeted me, "Ms. Hamilton is finished evaluating your papers, you may come in and go to her office she is waiting for you." My heart began to throb with confident expectation. Approaching Ms. Hamilton's office I knocked on the door. Ms. Hamilton said, "Come in". Smiling, she said, "I have read your testimony, statement of belief, and evaluated your test scores. Based on the interviews that I have performed all day I have selected you to be our next Counselor. However the next process in your interview will be to meet with Bishop Blum. I will make my recommendations to him, but he always reserves the privilege to make the final decision." She continued to tell me that Bishop was extremely busy, and she did not know when he'd be able to see me but it should be within two weeks as the Counseling department was in dire need due to backed-up appointments. In addition Ms. Hamilton informed me that the church's staff would be going on their annual retreat, and invited me to come with them. With a smile and sigh of relief, I told her "Thank you and I'd be looking forward to working with you."

When I left the office and got into my car, the praises came forth. I thanked the Lord throughout my entire ride home. When Jambila got home from school, I shared the good news with her. We praised the Lord together again. That evening we decided to eat dinner at an exclusive restaurant in Hollywood to celebrate what the Lord had done for us. By HIS gracious generosity towards me, HE confirmed my relocation by establishing me in stable employment in ministry.

During my orientation period I was informed of the importance of confidentiality, and the necessity of documentation. Basically I was thrown into an office to help serve a diverse group of people with numerous challenges. Prior to my appointment as a Counselor, I felt pretty sure that I had something to offer God's people. After sitting in the Counseling unit of the church for two weeks, most of the times I was at a complete loss as to what should be said to God's people.

Sometimes I would ride home in complete amazement at the enormity and significance of the task that was put in my trust. I learned quickly to rely on the word of God. I learned to listen actively, I asked the Lord to develop more of a prayer life in me, if I was to be used to help HIS people. Reliance on God's word and HIS counsel was predominant in my counseling. It did not matter what I thought or what I felt like telling the counselee. If God's word said it, that is what I believed and said.

Adopting the skill of active listening was absolutely necessary in this field. I've always been the one to run off at the mouth but I was taught by the Holy Spirit to listen. Listen attentively to what the counselee is saying, as well as listen for directives from the Holy Spirit as to what questions should be asked. Listening to what the client was not saying. Being slow to speak, but quick to listen. Of all the skills that HE sharpened me with, to be an effective Counselor, listening and not saying anything was the most difficult. Prayer without ceasing became a way of life as I listened to the different types of problems, uncertainties and questions. Prayer was essential to me in hearing from the Holy Spirit, and in keeping my fleshly thoughts and opinions from intervening. Prayer was the key to the maintenance of my emotional well-being.

In My Jerusalem

O ne morning I was awakened by the telephone ringing. Mae, had called to tell me that Mother had gone into the hospital to have surgery, and while on the operating table, she had suffered a stroke that immobilized her left hand and left arm and she was unable to speak. Alarmed, I asked Mae a series of questions! "Is she conscious? Is she able to recognize you? What is the doctor saying? How long will she be hospitalized? Does the doctor recommend speech therapy, physical therapy?" Mae told me that she and the doctors didn't know to what extent the stroke had damaged Mother's ability to think, speak, walk, or remember. However, a brain scan has been ordered to be administered within a few days. From what Mae was telling me, I concluded that after the brain scan was done the doctor would be able to determine what her chances of recovery were from the stroke.

Hanging up the telephone I began to cry and became frantic with concern for my Mother's well-being. I was afraid that perhaps this illness would end in her death. Crying, I fell on my knees and began to intercede on her behalf. I prayed that the Lord would restore her health, I prayed that the Lord would not permit her to suffer any long-term disabilities from this illness. I prayed for all of her caretakers at the hospital. I prayed that I'd be able to take care of her after her rehabilitation period. I prayed that my sisters would be in agreement with Mother relocating to Los Angeles. I prayed that when she arrived in Los Angeles we would have sufficient to meet her every need. I prayed for a reputable, reliable person to be sent across my path to be loving and compassionate towards Mother while I worked. I prayed for everything that came to my mind. I was real glad that the Lord understood my pitiful babblings. I believed that HE heard them and answered every request. When I got through praying, as I got up off my knees,

148

the last thing I said was, "Lord, not my will but YOUR will be done."

The days that followed Mae's phone call were filled with fears, and worry, and hopelessness. Every time the telephone rang, I anticipated some one being on the other end of the line giving me bad news about my Mother. Each day was difficult, it was hard for me to remain focused on the work at hand. My thoughts were consumed with questions. Should I take leave from my job to travel to New Orleans? Not being in the very place where Mother lived, able to see her with my own eyes was hard to bear. I wanted to be with her so that I could make a determination not based on someone else's insight.

At this point I had to rely totally on the Lord for directions. This was a time of intense prayer and consecration for me. It was imperative for me to know what the mind of the Holy Spirit was in this matter with my Mother. So I continued in prayer. It appeared to me that the more I prayed the more of HIS peace I experienced. This peace was not predicated on the fact that I heard that it was well with my Mother. But this peace was a peace that came from the throne of GOD, that HE was in control and HE and HE alone was causing me to learn to trust and rest in HIM.

Jambila and I had been renting a house in South Los Angeles for the past three years. Even though it was only Jambila and myself, our house had three bedrooms, two full baths, living/dining room, kitchen, and family room. While in between jobs I decided to obtain a license to open a home for the many children in the Los Angeles County Department of Children Services that needed good loving homes. The licensing process included orientation and certification. Orientation was a six week process to educate prospective foster parents son how to handle the discipline, and the psychological, and emotional problems that one would occasionally encounter. Certification involved more extensive training if you were to foster children that had special needs.

After being terminated from employment in property management, for the second time, I decided to seek employment that was not intricately related to my housing needs. Perhaps I was too proficient in bringing a property from low or no occupancy to 100% occupancy. I began contract work with the City of Los Angeles Housing Authority as a Human Resource Analyst. This work was very challenging as well as an educational experience for me. I was responsible for recruitment, testing, benefits, orientation, and training for all classified employees.

After successfully completing all the requirements that the County of Los Angeles mandated for foster parents, I received my first placement. He was a seven day old boy that was born addicted to cocaine. These babies were referred to as "crack babies." They required additional care in that their little bodies would react to the foreign substance that their Mothers used while she was carrying them. They did not bond easily, some had severe respiratory deficiencies. Withdrawal was very common among these babies, they cried excessively, and some either had extremely good appetites, or no appetite at all.

When I was contacted as to whether I would take this child in my foster home, I had many questions for the Children Services Social Worker. " Where was the Mother? Where was the Father or the other closely related family members? Did the Mother or Father have visiting privileges? Were there any other medical needs that the child had?" The Social Worker explained to me that the mother of this baby had abandoned him at the hospital. She was on probation from a previous felony charge. Since the baby was born with cocaine in his system, the courts viewed that as a violation of probation and she would probably have to go back to prison.

The Mother evidently knew this and became fearful and abandoned the baby in the hospital. She did not even take the time to name the baby. When he was placed with me the only name he had was baby boy Peidmon. Within two weeks, the

150

social worker called to say that she had found the mother, and she wanted the baby named Jason. I distinctively remember going to Martin Luther King Hospital, identifying myself, showing pictured ID to the nurse's station. Obviously, the nursing staff had been alerted to release the baby to my custody. For a few minutes I reflected on the special times when I brought my own babies home from the hospital. Right before the baby was due, I always spent a special day to shop for clothing for my newborn baby to wear on his/her trip home.

There I stood in the hallway, where no special arrangements had been made for this little boy. The only fanfare he encountered was to be abandoned by his mother, and to be taken to the home of a stranger. There was no special clothing for him. No one had lovingly, meticulously selected clothes for him to wear. Hurriedly, the nurse requested me to sign the release for baby boy Peidmon to leave the hospital. Swiftly, another nurse handed me a small package of formula and disposable diapers. Then I was handed the baby, wrapped in two hospital issue receiving blankets. Armed with a newborn baby only seven days old, I walked to the elevator. I removed the receiving blanket to take my first look at the baby that I would nurture.

Tears welled up in my eyes as I looked on this perfectly precious creation of God. Perfectly formed, he had all his fingers and toes. Jason was dressed in a hospital issue undershirt and a disposable diaper. He had a head full of light brown hair, and was asleep like a precious little angel. As I walked to my car my mind went back again to the times when

I brought my babies home from the hospital. There was always someone at home to greet us, with a showy reception of love and well wishes. I reflected on the two-am feedings, colic, and just plain fussy babies.

In order for me to continue my employment without interruption, it was necessary for me to hire a caretaker for Jason. One of the churches in Los Angeles provided a placement

151

service for Hispanics who did either domestic or carpentry work. After interviewing several applicants, I decided to hire a middle age female from El Salvador, to take care of Jason and to perform domestic duties. I was finally in a position to hire someone to do the jobs that previously only I had performed.

My mind wandered to the times when I wished that there were a husband in the home to assist with the good, bad, and ugly times of rearing my children. The times when we had very little food and I suggested to my kids that we have a candle light party. The truth was we had very little food in the house except bread, cold cuts, a half-bag of stale potato chips, and Kool-Aid. The candles supplied light to the dining room because the electricity had been shut off. Sometimes there was not enough money to pay the electricity and gas bills. The times when we had to get by on meager fare, better known as welfare. The times when I'd weep all night long wondering how could I provide for some additional need that the kids school was requesting. The times when I was so stressed out due to the pressures of parenting I considered running away. The times when I thought that death was a pleasant option and escape. The times when I've walked over two miles to get to work and then stood on my feet for eight hours, only to walk the two miles home at the end of the day.

Jarred back from my preoccupation by Jason's soft cries and squirming, I pulled into the driveway of our house. Jambila ran out of the gate to the car to assist me with our baby. She was overcome with love for Jason at the first look. She unstrapped him from his confines in the car seat and began talking very softly, commenting on how handsome he was. "Mama," she said, "How long can we keep him? He is so cute! I don't know Jambi, his Mom left him in the hospital, so I guess it will be for a short period of time until his Mama can get herself together again." That was the beginning of a service that we provided in our home for over ten years. During the course of that time we fostered over twenty-one children.

Jambila was a tremendous help; she was the big sister to all the children that went through my foster care. She combed hair, gave baths, escorted to amusement parks, walked to school, and even baby sat with the kids while I either took another child for a medical appointment or just needed to take a night off. Jambila always wanted a little sister or brother. She missed her older siblings a lot. She even jokingly commented to me, "I did want a little brother or sister but this is ridiculous!" The children loved Jambila and she loved them right back.

Eventually, the Department of Children & Family Services would permit the parents to come to the home to have supervised visits with their children. This afforded me an opportunity to become more familiar with the parents, as well as an open door to share my belief in Jesus Christ.

During my tenure as a foster parent I had the privilege of nurturing abused, neglected, abandoned, drug-dependent, emotionally disturbed, physically challenged, sexually molested, and medically needy children back to a healthy, wholesome mind and body. Some of these children had experienced some adverse situations that I, as an older adult had not ever encountered in my entire life. All I wanted them to experience in their short lived lives was to enjoy their lives as children.

Whenever a reunion with the child's parents took place, I was both happy and saddened. Saddened that my time with that particular child was ended but happy to see the confident look on their parent's faces as they came to reclaim their children and bring them back to their homes.

Parenting, foster parenting, and holding a full-time job kept me quite busy. However, there was still an emptiness that kept gnawing at me, a feeling that I could be, and perhaps should be, doing more. This uneasiness caused me to pray and ask for directives from the Holy Spirit as to what else could I do? I was very much aware of the danger of becoming overwhelmed and unbalanced. Unbalanced meaning not having enough time to spend with the Lord, or to rest, or for spending quality time with family members. In spite of all the many tasks that were already overloading my plate, I still longed to do more. I felt that I could do more I was not driven by guilt, but a longing to see the greater works that Jesus spoke of in St. John 14:12 "Most assuredly, I say to you, he who believes in ME, the works that I do he will do also, and greater works than these he will do, because I go to My Father."(NKJV)

After much prayer and waiting before the Lord, I felt impressed by the Holy Spirit to inquire with the Los Angeles Main County Jail. Having been interviewed by the Religious Director, fingerprinted, and my background investigated, I was approved to go in the County Jail to preach salvation to the men that were hospitalized. Escorted by the grace and favor of God, I was granted the privilege to proclaim the gospel to every prisoner on the fourth tier that was ambulatory. We were permitted to use the dining area to accommodate all of the inmates. There was one encounter with an inmate that has been indelibly imprinted in my mind.

At check in, I would go immediately to an office that had been set aside by the Los Angeles County Sheriff's Department to counsel the inmates. Sometimes the inmates just desired to have time out of their cells. Others had received Jesus Christ as their Savior, and due to the prison regulations, could not respond to the invitation to discipleship as we do in our traditional churches. In the corporate worship services in the Prison Chapel the inmates were encouraged to request counseling and to share with one of the counselors their decision to accept Jesus as Lord. It was during these times that we had an opportunity to issue Bibles and other Christian literature.

Specifically, I remember having talked to this particular inmate who had accepted Jesus as his Lord. I remember him because of his sharing with me in prior sessions that he needed special prayers because he was being transported to a maximum security facility within a couple of weeks. He came every day to get instructions from the Word of God, and to talk with the Chaplains. He had so many questions, and he wanted to take advantage of the opportunity to counsel with Godly men and women.

At service I preached a message that exhorted the men to ask the Lord in prayer what was HIS purpose for their lives. To find a place in HIM that they could serve HIM, even behind bars. The Holy Spirit encouraged those men to be an example that Christ was in their lives, in word and deed. After that service was over I began gathering my Bible to go home. The word came to the Chaplain's office that a group of men were being bussed out to another facility. Normally, I did not respond to this type of information, it was commonplace for inmates to be bussed out to other prisons. But this time, I especially felt a tug in my heart that I desired to say goodbye to the regular attendees of the worship service.

Armed with nothing other than compassion for these young men I proceeded to the lower level. As I approached the lower level. I observed that the Sheriff was already leading a group of prisoners to board the bus that would transport them to another house of detention. I requested the Deputy's permission to just say goodbye to the inmates. The Deputy granted my request.

As I went down the line bidding goodbye and God bless you to each of the shackled prisoners, I noticed the one convert who had this insatiable desire to know more about his relationship with Jesus. I looked at him and held back the tears that were welling up in my eyes. I just told him, "Brother I know that the Lord will use you mightily in HIS kingdom through your obedience to the word, your lifestyle, and your sharing your faith in Jesus Christ." By this time the inmate had begun to weep openly, and said to me, " Preacher lady, you did not know this but I prayed last night and asked the Lord to put it in your mouth what HE wanted me to do for HIM since He has done so much for me." We both understood what had happened as we stood staring at each other weeping as the prisoners and the Deputies looked on in total wonder.

Twice weekly I continued to visit the prisoners, and bring the "GOOD NEWS" to them. Through my counseling I learned about the many challenges an incarcerated person faces, after his release from prison. Foremost, their concerns were housing, and employment. As I began to seek the Lord as to what part HE'D have me to play in this difficulty, I felt impressed to start a food ministry to the homeless of downtown Los Angeles. With no resources I began to purchase food and cook it for the homeless people.

My first time feeding downtown, I was assisted by my family members. We cooked a large pot of red beans w/rice seasoned with smoked turkey necks, corn bread, green salad, and canned soda pop. We were able to feed approximately fifty persons. I was elated to be able to help fill the gap in a very small manner; however I was heartsick to see so many that had to be turned away because we did not have enough to feed all that had lined up on the street. That experience thrust me into requesting donations and volunteers to assist with the feeding of the homeless. Fortunately, most of the people contacted either volunteered food or donated money. As a result of God's amazing grace, we were able to feed downtown weekly over one hundred and fifty hot home cooked meals. In the midst of full-time employment, weekly home Bible studies, foster parenting, the feeding ministry, and the prison ministry still another service was soon added for me to perform.

I kept in touch with Mae and her news about Mother's progress since her stroke. On one occasion I spoke with Mother's physician, Dr. Levy. He informed me that Mother was doing well, her speech had returned and he would talk with Mae regarding placing her in a rehabilitation hospital. His goal for Mother was that she learn to walk again, to dress herself and perform simple personal hygiene tasks with the use of her right hand. Dr. Levy informed me that, possibly with intensive therapy Mother could get some usage out of her left arm and hand, but he said the rehabilitation would be minimum. The duration of the physical therapy was to be eight weeks. After the eight weeks were over, Mae told me that Dr. Levy wanted to try another six to eight weeks therapy on Mother. Pat, Mae, and I all agreed with Dr. Levy's extended therapy. Mae was excellent about keeping her siblings informed about Mother's condition. Pat was now living in Michigan, I in Los Angeles. Mae was the only daughter left in New Orleans. We discussed Mother's discharge with the Social Worker at the rehab hospital. After much prayer we three sisters decided that I would travel to New Orleans to retrieve Mother to live with me after her physical therapy sessions were completed.

Finally when Mother was released from the rehabilitation hospital, I traveled to New Orleans to relocate her to Los Angeles. Having made arrangements with the moving company prior to leaving Los Angeles, I anticipated my trip would go smoothly. Basically I was to arrive in New Orleans on one day, the same day that I had coordinated with the moving company to pick up Mother's things. I was so glad to see my Mother. Physically she was doing well, except her left arm still lacked firmness due to the severity of the stroke she had suffered. It was planned that Mother and I were to take a hotel room late the same evening of the day of my arrival. We chose to book a hotel that was in proximity to the New Orleans International Airport so we could take the hotel's shuttle to the airline. We were blessed that everything worked out as planned.

Becoming the caretaker for my Mother proved to be disarraying, delightful and despairing. We were still living in the three-bedroom, living/dining room, kitchen, family room, and two bath house that we had rented in South Los Angeles when Mother came to live with us. At that time, Leah, and Alaina two siblings were also in my foster care. Jason, my very first foster child was four months old.

157

Jason and I slept in the Master bedroom, Jambila had her own bedroom, and Leah and Alaina shared the third bedroom. When Mother arrived with all of her clothing, personal items, and furniture we were plunged into total disorder. Where to put all these additional items, furnishings, and clothing became a major issue. Even sleeping arrangements were adjusted to accommodate Mother and her things. I rearranged people, clothing and furniture. Mother was quite adamant about not getting rid of her things. As I reflect back on her decision and realize how attached I'd become to my personal items, I understood. Mother probably figured it is enough that I am uprooted from my environment, my church, all the people who I've grown to love, my home for over forty five years, and now you are requesting me to give up these few things that are reminiscent of better times in my life? I think not!

We finally came up with a workable plan. Jambila moved Jason's crib into her room, Mother moved in my room, Leah and Alaina remained in their current room. Their places were secured due to regulations by the Department of Children and Family Services. Jason's sleeping arrangements could be changed. Because he was under two years of age he could sleep in his crib, in a room with another child or adult.

Closet space was extremely limited in this house. When this house was built, obviously the builder did not anticipate Mary Bradshaw's wardrobe. Mother has always been a meticulous, fashion-conscious dresser. So there were many dresses, suits, hats, shoes, purses, overcoats, full-length mink overcoats, fox stoles with hats. My closet was already stuffed to capacity and overflowed into the family room's guest closet. Finally I determined that the rest of Mother's personal items and furniture would have to be carefully stored in the family room until we could find a larger house to live in.

Mother enjoyed going to bed early. I preferred looking at the eleven o'clock news on television, reading the paper and some Bible prior to retiring. Mother possessed the ability to awaken at 5:00 in the morning. Whereas I favored sleeping until the last minute, then running madly through out the house to ensure everyone was up, washed, combed and fed prior to going out for school. It was our normal procedure for the kids to use the second bathroom as they knew it was my custom to getup at the last minute rushing. However, my dear Mother would monopolize the master bathroom while she did her devotional reading and prayers. Consequently, we had to make greater adjustments to our schedules so that I would not be late for work. Eventually, the disarray became orderly and we adjusted to the changes and enjoyed Mother's stay with us.

Delightful cannot fully describe the times I shared with Mother. She was a faithful friend, confidante, travel companion, and shopping buddy. On the occasions that I had preaching engagements, I could count on Mother to be there. I think the part that she took pleasure in most was when I introduced her to the church/audience. I would say, " I am so pleased to have here with me today my friend, and faithful follower, my Mother." She would stand before the church, waving and throwing kisses to them. I believe she particularly enjoyed this because a worship service normally had about two thousand parishioners, and she loved the attention and spotlight.

Mother was an excellent counselor. She always listened very intently as I shared some of the intimate details of my life. She would never condemn me; however she did not condone my unwise choices.

Choices that I made regarding relationships with men, choices that I executed in disciplining my children. Even though my sisters and I were disciplined at times by corporeal punishment, Mother didn't condone this for grands to be disciplined in a like manner. She would often appeal to me on behalf of the kids.

The few times that I dated, I'd always bring my date in to meet my family. It was during these times that I met a man who was a retired physician. As I usually did with dates, I had him to pick me up from our home. Mother was sitting in her wheelchair, richly dressed in her pink satin nightgown and bed jacket. I said "Mother this is George and he is from West Virginia." Looking up at him from her chair with those beautyful big brown eyes she responded, " Good to meet you, Pansy is this the Doctor that you been making all the fuss over?" Embarrassed I said, "Yes Mother this is Doctor Rutk in." She quickly responded, "He certainly doesn't look like a physician to me, he looks like any other Joe Blow from off the street to me." By this time Jambila, Mother's caretaker Maria, Leah, and Alaina, were about to smother attempting to hold back the laughter.

Mortified, hurriedly I left last minute instructions for Maria, and Jambila while apologizing to George at the same time. Mother's appetite left a lot to be desired. The foods that her physician recommended her to eat she refused, simply stating the food was too bland. Frustrated, I'd ask her, "What do you want to eat?" Normally I kept a well-stocked pantry and freezer but Mother would always request an item of food that I did not keep. One evening she wanted Lobster, another time she desired pizza, and still another time she wanted turtle soup. On this particular evening she desired to eat pizza. Jambila and I jumped in the car and proceeded to the pizza place. When we arrived back at home I prepared Mother a slice of pizza and a salad. She took one bite of the pizza and complained, "It's too greasy and too cheesy!" Jambila and I looked at each other and roared in laughter. Mother had to join us as she realized that she had requested this pizza and now it was too greasy and too cheesy. There were times that she slipped in and out of dementia, but most of the times her mental capabilities were clear and concise.

Jambila was enrolled in college, and holding a part-time job with a major grocery chain as a cashier. She had begun dating a young man a tour church named Ben. Ben was a fine young man from Christian parents.

One afternoon Jambila invited one of her co-workers home to meet her family, his name was Abe. Mother, and Jambila were all sitting in the family room when Abe arrived. Jambila made the introductions to Mother and I. I was busy in the kitchen, Mother keep repeating this young man's name. "Abe? Abe?" Abe began to pay attention to her. She then said, "Abe? Abe Lincoln, whatever happened to Ben Franklin?" Quickly, I realized that Mother was referring to the young man that Jambila had been seeing Ben. With an attempt to distract her or throw her off course, I responded, "Oh Mother are you associating Abe's name with the sixteenth president of the United States?" She did not respond. Jambila and I looked at each other, knowing very well to whom she was referring to. The first time that Mother met Ben she immediately took a special liking to him. I think in her mind she considered Ben the type of person she desired Jambila to be with.

As I continued preparing the meal for the night, I offered Abe, Jambila, and Mother some lemonade. Mother refused, Jambila and Abe accepted. While I was placing the tray of glasses and pitcher of lemonade on the table, Mother started again calling Abe's name, "Abe? Abe?" Choosing to ignore her prattle, I intervened, "You like Abe's name huh?" She finally said, "Abe? Abe Lincoln, where is Ben Franklin? Get lost Abe, Ben Franklin is here! Get lost Abe." This time Jambila laughingly said tome "Maybe your Mother is tired and wants to go to bed." Mother continued to prattle, "Get lost Abe, get lost Abe." Inconspicuously, I made light of her insults to the young man, and rolled her wheel chair to her room. After Abe left, Jambila and I joked about Mother's comment to the man she considered an intruder and her unique way of telling him that Jambila was seeing a guy named Ben.

Finally we moved into a house that would comfortably accommodate all of the family. My real estate agent had been unsuccessful in locating a house that would provide a bedroom for Mother, a separate bedroom for Jambila, and two additional bedrooms for my adopted daughters and foster children.

While sitting at work on a rare rainy day, I was contacted by the real estate agent and informed that he had two houses that could serve our family needs. After canceling my appointments for the remainder of the day, I met Bradley at a house located in Beverly Hills. Bradley was a very easygoing man I'd met through one of my clients at the church. His willing-ness to allow me to go through most of his listings, to meet me to show a house when the property was listed with another realty company, and his going out of his way to serve my needs at a moments notice were qualities that I had not found in other real estate agents.

Driving up to the house as I saw the place had curb appeal. The lawn was finely landscaped and trimmed. The house was freshly painted. Bradley had arrived before me, and was on his cell phone obtaining the code so that we could gain access to the vacant house. "How are things going?", he said. I answered, "Fine". Bradley always asked about Mother and the children. "Mother and the children are fine. I am the one that is still being challenged due to cramped quarters." He responded, "Hang in there with me kid I will find suitable housing for you and the family." As we entered through the front door we were in a huge living/dining room combination with the kitchen straight ahead, to the right were the bedrooms. Immediately I took off to inspect the bedrooms. I am a stickler for closets, and adequate closet space. As I continued my visual inspect-ion, I noticed there were no closets in three of the bedrooms. I questioned Bradley, his response was, "I'll call my office and find out what's the story." I had inspected houses enough to know that a room could not officially be considered as a bedroom unless there was a closet.

Bradley talked with his office, he told me that this house had been previously used as an office and renovated to remove all of the original closets. I was a little agitated with Bradley that he had not done his homework prior to pulling me from my office to show a house that was legally a two-bedroom house with a lot of additional rooms in it. Bradley suspected that I was disturbed and informed me that he had seen this next house, but he had to call the listing agent's office to obtain the code to gain entry into the property.

By this time I could no longer conceal my ire and I said, "Bradley didn't you inspect these listings prior to calling me from my office? I took the remainder of the day off just to see these properties and I'm finding that they do not meet the needs of my family nor have you researched or viewed these listings! I am not interested in being on a wild goose chase." Quickly Bradley responded, "If you'll come to see this one I know you'll like it. Please give me another chance." "Did you get an opportunity to inspect this property? Or is this another wild goose chase? Frankly Bradley, I am quite displeased because I took off from work, will miss a half day pay and you are not even showing me homes that will fit my family's needs."

Reluctantly I went to the address Bradley provided me with and I was sure he was showing me another hacked-up shack. I wondered in my mind, I've been in Los Angeles now for the better part of eight years and have never heard of Lorraine Boulevard. After following Bradley on a five-minute-drive from the other address, we stopped in front of what appeared from the outside to be a huge house.

We were on a narrow street that had several two-story Mediterranean—some custom built, some Tudor estates on both sides of the street. The lawns were well manicured and the homes were all well maintained. I was not impressed. Bradley was still in his automobile with his cell phone to his ear. As the rain fell more heavily, my patience was wearing thin. Finally, Bradley got out of his car, and came to the window of my car. " Bradley you are not prepared to show this home, right? No, he responded, "as a matter of fact I just got off the phone with the realty company, and we can obtain access." "Which one of the houses is it, I asked? The light pink one with the awnings." Looking up I saw a two-story stucco estate with an upgraded curved pavement that led to oversized double mahogany doors. The doors had beveled glass in the upper portion, and a deep brown mahogany hue on the lower half. The exterior of the house was freshly painted a pale dusty rose pink, trimmed with white. The front porch had been painted the same white. On both sides of the entry door the windows were meticulously covered with a coordinating pale pink canvas scalloped awning, embroidered at the bottom with thick white threads and tassels. The style of house was Mediterranean, possibly built between the nineteen thirties and forties.

Even though the house had curb appeal, I was still skeptical due to my previous experience earlier with Bradley. I had viewed a house that externally was appealing but the inside of the house left much to be desired. We walked up to the entry and Bradley entered the combination for access to the property. Bradley opened the door and I walked in.

Upon entering the first thing I noticed was the highly buffed and shiny dark brown wood floors that lit up the entry hall. On the right hand side was a huge living room with a fireplace, the walls were painted white, the floors in the living room were carpeted in a mauve colored carpeting that would match my furniture. The ceilings were highlighted with crown moldings and recessed lighting. Across the entry hallway was a dining room that was separated from the entry hall by glass double doors, the floors were the same beautifully buffed wood floors as the entry hallway. I was amazed. I returned to the entry hallway and began to walk the length of the hall. Facing me were two louvered white doors.

At this point a very unusual confidence came over me. Without asking Bradley about the selling price, how many bedrooms, bathrooms, etc., I told Bradley, "This is the house, I will purchase this house." Bradley looked at me and said "Are you sure? You have not seen the rest of the house nor have you asked the listing price." Confidently, I assured Bradley that whatever the listing price, "God would provide all of my needs". Smiling he looked at me and responded, "Perhaps you'd better look at the house that God has just provided for you just to make sure it has all the amenities that you need." Laughing at his remarks, I told him "Bradley you will see the hand of God move on our behalf for this house."

Continuing towards those white louvered doors, I passed the stairway to the second level of the house. The double doors opened into a huge kitchen and family room that ran the entire rear width of the house. In the back yard was a sparkling pool that was surrounded by a six-foot iron gate. Perfect, I thought, for my foster children. Attached to the family room was a huge kitchen with built-ins. As I explored the kitchen, there was a doorway that led to an inside utility room, and behind the utility room there was a full bathroom and a medium sized bedroom with a closet. At this point my heart began to flutter with anticipation. The bedroom/bathroom area on the first floor was ideal for Mother. Mother had begun to be restless at night and her restlessness affected the entire family and kept us from sleeping.

Upstairs was a master suite with a master bathroom with adjoining bath, four other bedrooms, and another bathroom. This house possessed more than adequate space for me and my family. In total there were six bedrooms, three full baths, formal living room, formal dining room, family room, and kitchen.

Later, as Bradley and I sat down with Mother to submit a written offer for acquisition of the house, Bradley affirmed what I suspected. We had sufficient money for the down payment if the offer was accepted, but we were lacking several thousand dollars for the closing costs. Mother at this point told Bradley, "We'll have the required money for closing when it is necessary." With that assurance Bradley left with the agreement to purchase as well as a check for the down payment. The agreement to purchase had a contingency that required the seller to respond within seventy-two hours or the offer would be counted as invalid.

When Bradley left I discussed with Mother where I would get the additional money if the offer was accepted. Looking at me skeptically, she said, "Jesus has provided for us all this way and He will provide every thing that we need". Even though she was not present when I spoke similar words to Bradley, it was if the Holy Ghost was mirroring my words back to me. Fear began to knock on my door, but I chose not to answer its call, realizing who was in control, not Mother's bank account, not the seller of the real estate property, and certainly not my inadequacies. This situation would prove to be a fertile ground for trust and faith issues to be nurtured.

By day two, Bradley called me with an acceptance of our offer to purchase the house. He informed me that the seller wanted us to close escrow as soon as possible. I called the bank, and the wheels of finance and closure of escrow went into action.

The next week I was contacted by the escrow company and informed that the seller wanted me to assume the loan he had recently obtained, he was not asking for a down payment, all we had to do was qualify for the loan. As I explained this to Mother we both rejoiced in that the Lord had intervened in our situation and had heard and answered our prayers. The several thousand dollar check that I had written to be utilized as a down payment would now be used as closing costs and the need for additional money was no longer necessary.

Within three weeks we had qualified for the loan and closed escrow. We were refunded money from the down payment check because the closing costs were minimum as we closed escrow towards the end of the month. We used the additional money to defray the costs of moving.

Subsequently, we moved into our new home that would comfortably house all of my family with room to spare. Mother occupied the downstairs bedroom. Due to her bouts with irrationality, her room needed to be accessible to the nursing staff that served her daily.

In the old house we had been cramped and uncomfortable. In the new house we had two guests bedroom and we were very comfortable.

Mother's condition had grown markedly worse, and in the nighttime she would call out to me to assist her to walk to the restroom. Finally, after many nights of broken rest, I explained to her that her options were to have a catheter placed in her bladder, or to wear underwear for people who were incontinent. All of my suggestions were responded to negatively. So I asked her what did she want me to do, explaining the difficulty that I was experiencing in not getting a full night's sleep. Reluctantly, Mother agreed to wear the incontinent underwear. I realized her hesitancy to agree to any of the options that I suggested, she interpreted them as her losing her freedom. Even though she agreed to wearing the special underwear she would still rattle the rails of her bed and call out for me to come and change her bed clothing. So the interrupted sleep patterns continued. No matter how much I explained to Mother, she would still yell for me in the middle of the night.

Leah and Alaina shared adjoining bedrooms with Jambila. I occupied the master suite and we had two remaining upstairs bedrooms that were unoccupied. Mother occupied the only downstairs bedroom. Periodically, through the night I would go downstairs to check on Mother.

Mother had nurses and aides that would come to the house Sundays through Saturday. Their duties were to change her bed linen, to bathe her, take her vital signs, administer medications, shampoo and comb her hair, vacuum the carpet in her room, and clean her bathroom.

It was necessary for me to hire a housekeeper/caretaker after we moved into our new home. Again the local church had an employment service which I used to locate a suitable person to take care of Mother. Maria, a petite, young immigrant from Tijuana, Mexico was the one that I selected. I picked Maria, because she loved Jesus Christ. Her very little experience with the English language made it difficult for mother or I to effectively communicate. However, the language of love transcended any spoken language barriers. With the little English she did speak Maria told me, "I love Jesus Christ!" I hadn't even asked her about her religious background. In the middle of conversation with the interpreter, she blurted out, " I love Jesus Christ!" I told the interpreter to tell Maria she had the job, and that my main priority was that she takes good care of my Mother. Maria was excellent with Mother, as though she was caring for her firstborn infant.

What a joy it was to have everyone have their own space and Mother taken care of with the love, patience and kindness that she deserved. Even though the housing issue had been settled, I still could see Mother's condition degenerating. I worked less than five minutes from where I resided. Fortunately, Maria was perceptive enough to get me on the telephone at work when Mother became ill, in spite of her being unpolished in the English language.

Mother's bouts with small strokes called TIA"S (transient isochronal attacks) were frequent. Her personal physician explained to me that these were small strokes that occurred because the arteries that transported blood to her brain were closing because they were clogged with fatty deposits. Whenever I received the dreaded call from Maria, I would become panic-stricken, rush out of the office, drive up Crenshaw Boulevard at lightning speed, praying and binding the enemy throughout the entire drive. Sometimes I arrived at the same time as the paramedics.

I remember one crisis when I had been summoned from my office by Maria, and when I arrived at home I found Mother unconscious in the shower stall on the floor. I had already called the paramedics before I left my office. My heart stopped beating as I saw my dear Mother. She appeared to be dead. Immediately I knelt down and took her head in my lap. I began to speak to that spirit of infirmity. "In the name of Jesus I command you to leave her body, she shall not die but live, to declare the works of the Lord. She is healed by HIS stripes, and I will bless the Lord O my soul and we will not forget all of HIS benefits, who heals all manner of diseases!" Suddenly, as if she had been awakened from sleep, Mother eyes fluttered and opened with her saying, "Hi Pansy, did I fall in the shower?" By the time the paramedics arrived there was no need to transport her to the hospital, the GREAT PHYSICIAN had touched her body.

Each morning as I awakened I was afraid to walk downstairs, dreading that Mother would not be alive. When, after mature consideration, I realized that this was a spirit of fear, I prayed, and the Lord delivered me. Thoughts of being without Mother in my life caused me to be very despondent. However, as I meditated on God's promises, the fear of death diminished and was inevitably eliminated through faith in HIS word. Despairing as those thoughts were, I had to continue loving, and caring for my Mother. It was extremely difficult for me to see her failing health, her lack of appetite, her gaunt body, hear her slurred speech, and observe irrationality take over her intellect.

Mother was a dignified woman with impeccable taste, posture, intelligence and could articulate very well with her limited eighth grade education. Whenever I observed her in this weakened state I felt very sorrowful and unable to help her. I knew that I was doing all that was humanly possible for me to make her comfortable. Eventually, these emotions of incompetence prompted me to seek God's face as to what else could I do for my Mother.

The Holy Spirit responded, "Talk to her about her salvation, about whether or not she was fearful of dying?" I was reluctant to discuss death with Mother for I did not know how she would interpret the conversation. When I finally mustered enough courage, to approach her, I treaded delicately. I approached her room silently, while saying a prayer and asking God for wisdom, tact, and grace.

When I reached the doorway to her room she lifted her hand for me to take as she usually did. "How do you feel, Mother, is there anything hurting you, do you want something to eat or drink?"

"I feel fine, there is nothing hurting me, and I am not hungry or thirsty."

"Will you take a little water anyway?" Noticing her catheter bag it held a small amount of fluid, she consented to taking a couple of swallows of water and then motioned to me with a hand up that she had enough. While pulling up a chair to her bedside, I said, "Mother tell me about your salvation experience.

"You mean when the Lord saved my soul from an eternally burning hell?"

"Yes, Mother, tell me how the Lord saved you." Her eyes brightened as she began to remember. "When I was a very young girl around ten years old, I began praying and asking the Lord to give me religion. In those days you were instructed by the older folks to pray, and the Lord would give you a sign. Then you would have to go to speaking meeting to tell the elders what sign the Lord had given you. If the elders discerned that you didn't have religion, they would tell you to go back and pray again. I didn't want to be embarrassed so I prayed and I prayed earnestly. I can still remember what I asked Jesus, I asked HIM, Lord I believe in you, and I believe that you died for me, and I need a sign that you have heard me and saved my soul from a burning Hell.

For the first week, I didn't hear anything from the Lord, and I prayed ever more earnestly. Revival was going on at the Mount Moriah Baptist Church in Abend, Louisiana and we had to attend church services every night. Most of the other converts for baptism had either visions or dreams, but I still did not hear a word from the Lord. I was beginning to get a little frustrated and desperate as I knelt down in my Mama's bedroom and prayed. I said Lord if you have saved me from a burning Hell, let it start to rain. I finished my prayers and got up and walked towards the kitchen. Before I reached the kitchen the rain began to pour down real hard on the corrugated tin roof of our house.

"Mother, was it cloudy or beginning to rain before your prayer?" "No, the sun had been shining brightly with no clouds or indication of rain. Well, you know we lived in the country part of Louisiana and scattered showers would come in an instant, so just to verify if that was the Lord or coincidence, I prayed again and said, Lord if you have truly heard my prayer and saved me, then make the rain to stop. Well sure enough the rain stopped just as soon as I stopped praying, and I knew that the Lord Jesus Christ had not only heard but answered my prayers, and HE had saved me."

I listened intently, as she related her salvation experience to me. She continued, "Yea, baby, the Lord saved me many years ago and I have been serving, and worshipping HIM for many years." Continuing in the same line of thought, I said, "Mother, I'd like to share some scriptures with you, do you mind if I read them now?" Shaking her head she said, "No, read on." My strategy was to engage her in interpretation of what the word of God states regarding death. I started reading from II Corinthians 5:1-8; "For we know that if our earthly house, this tent, is destroyed we have a building from God, a house not made with hands, eternal in the heavens. For in this we groan, earnestly desiring to be clothed with our habitation which is from heaven, if indeed, having been clothed we shall not be found naked. For we who are in this tent groan, being burdened, not because we want to be unclothed, but further clothed that mortality may be swallowed up by life. Now HE who has prepared us for this very thing is God, who also has given us the Spirit as a guarantee. So we are always confident, knowing that while we are at home in the body, we are absent from the Lord. For we walk by faith, not by sight. We are confident, yes, well pleased rather to be absent from the body and to be present with the Lord."

I paused and asked, "Did you understand what I just read?" She nodded positively. While flipping through the pages of the Bible again, I said, "Mother, there is one more scripture I'd like to read to you and then if you feel up to it we'll discuss these passages as they relate to us as believers in Jesus Christ." I began reading from St. John 14:1-4; "Let not your heart be troubled, you believe in God, believe also in ME. In my Father's house are many mansions; if it were not so, I would have told you, I go to prepare a place for you. And if I go and prepare a place for you, I will come again to receive you to MYSELF; that where I am, there you may be also. And where I go you know, and the way you know."

Before I could ask her any questions she began talking. "Pansy, I am fully prepared and waiting for Jesus to come and get me. HE has allowed me to live a full wonderful life here, but I know that I have a much better life awaiting me with HIM."

"Are you afraid of dying, Mother?"

"Absolutely not," she answered. "As I understand death it is a mere crossing from life as I know it here on earth, to be with the Lord. He has mansions prepared for me to live with HIM forever. You see I'll be gone with HIM, no more worries, no more pain, no more sickness, no more lack, but my concern right now is for my children and my grandchildren and for those who are coming after me. I can say as the Apostle Paul said, I have fought a good fight and finished my course, will you be able to say the same when the time for your departure is near?" That profound question went unanswered that day. I held her hand, and kissing her cheeks as she fell off asleep. She awakened enough to ask me to sing to her. "What song would you like me to sing to you Mother?" Very quietly she responded, " The Battle Hymn of the Republic!"

As I sat with Mother in her room, humming one of her favorite songs, I fought back the tears that were coming into my eyes. My heart was so full that I could hardly hum the song. Long after Mother had fallen sound asleep, I remained in her room holding and rubbing her hand. I realized that Mother would be going home to be with Jesus, but it was a fleeting thought that I rebuked instantly and forgot about. I had become so accustomed to disapproving thoughts that did not coincide with what I thought was the will of God, that I reprimanded the enemy mechanically. I reinforced my thought pattern with the word of God. I slowly tip toed out of Mother's room as not to awaken her.

On March 23, 1996 at 5:00 AM, Mother went home to be with the Lord. This spray of perfume was extremely bitter, and the fragrance lingers with me until this very day.

Reflecting back on my life, I remembered the wonderful times I'd spent with my family growing up as a child, the awful incident when I was battered by the white boys, the rejection and abuse suffered from the hands of a man I loved, the prejudices because I was dark complexioned, the favor that was shown because I had a God given talent to sing, the hurt, and pain of rejection, the mockery, sarcasm, that my children and I suffered because I was a single parent. Being misunderstood in the church family, being alienated and branded by the church family as being possessed by a "familiar spirit." The incidents of being wrongfully terminated, the bad choices I'd made in life, the consequences I've had to suffer as a result of sin, what was the purpose of these experiences?

I headed towards my bedroom upstairs. Before going upstairs, I checked the exterior doors to insure that the house was secure. As I turned in the living room to approach the stairs, I felt a tug in my heart to pray. I knelt in front of one of the green velvet chairs. As soon as my knees touched the floor the tears began to stream down my face. It was at times like these, when I came face to face with the King of Kings, that I could bare my soul, be and feel weak and defenseless. These

173

are the times that I allowed the real me to come forth and to literally strip myself before HIM. All of my inferior, awkward, inexperience, and emotions came spilling forth from my mouth. I really did not have a specific petition just someone that I could tell all was sufficient for me. Someone who could interpret all of the vain babbling, comprehend it, and provide the healing, guidance and support. That someone for me is Jesus.

After crying and praying to God for what appeared to be a lengthy period of time, I remained on my knees in the quietness of the living room, just luxuriating in the presence of the Lord. I began to hear a voice that distinctively was talking to me. The voice said, "You think I cannot use all the hidden past you've had? You wonder what is the purpose for the life that I have ordained for you, you do not see the relevancy, nor do you know the thoughts and plans that I have for you. When I ascended back on high to be seated on the right hand of my FATHER I diffused gifts to mankind so that they would be empowered to do the works that I did while I was on earth. Just as I diffused the Holy Spirit to the church, so have I smeared you with my fragrance. I have consecrated you for service unto ME. As the prophet, priest and kings were anointed for service for ME. I will use every experience that you've had to make a fragrance that uniquely smells of ME. Just as perfume clings to the person that it has been applied, so is it with this anointing that you will be scented with. As you go forth into all the world to preach the gospel to every creature, people of the world will know that you carry the sweet, fragrant, odor of the Holy Spirit, because you've been made odorous by the SWEET ROSE OF SHARON, THE LILY OF THE VALLEY!"

We can give thanks in everything And say,"Your will be done," For God's at work in everything To make us like His Son___D. DE Haan

Romans 8:28: And we know that all things work together for good, to them that love the Lord and are the called according to His purpose.

Colossians 1:24: I now rejoice in my sufferings for you, ... for the sake of His body, which is the church.

The suffering that we endure To bring light to a darkened soul; Gives great reason to rejoice. When lives, once broken, are made whole____Sper

II Corinthians 2:14: Now thanks be to God who always leads us in triumph in Christ, and through us diffuses the fragrance of HIS knowledge in every place. (NKJV)

BOOK AVAILABLE THROUGH

Milligan Books, Inc.

An Imprint of Professional Business Consulting Service

One More Spray of Perfume $13.95

Order Form

Milligan Books, Inc.

1425 W. Manchester Ave., Suite C, Los Angeles, CA 90047

(323) 750-3592

Name_____ Date _____

Address_____

City_____ State____ Zip Code _____

Day Telephone _____

Evening Telephone_____

Book Title_____

Number of books ordered___ Total..........$ _____

Sales Taxes (CA Add 8.25%.....................$ _____

Shipping & Handling $3.90 for one book..$ _____

Add $1.00 for each additional book..........$ _____

Total Amount Due....................................$ _____

% Check   % Money Order % Other Cards _____

% Visa   % MasterCard Expiration Date _____

Credit Card No. _____

Driver License No. _____

Make check payable to Milligan Books, Inc.

_____   _____

Signature   Date